A CAT CALLED DOG

JEM VANSTON

Matador
9 Priory Business Park
Kibworth Beauchamp
Leicestershire LE8 0RX, UK
Tel: (+44) 116 279 2299
Fax: (+44) 116 279 2277
Email: books@troubador.co.uk
Web: www.troubador.co.uk/matador

ISBN 978 1780885 599

British Library Cataloguing in Publication Data.
A catalogue record for this book is available from the British Library.

Typeset in Book Antiqua by Troubador Publishing Ltd
Printed and bound in the UK by TJ International, Padstow, Cornwall

Matador is an imprint of Troubador Publishing Ltd

'In nine lifetimes, you'll never know as much about your cat as your cat knows about you.'
Michel de Montaigne

'The smallest feline is a masterpiece.'
Leonardo da Vinci

'What greater gift than the love of a cat?'
Charles Dickens

'In a cat's eyes, all things belong to cats.'
English Proverb

AUTHOR NOTE

Many thanks to all those who have shown support for my writing over the years, and who have bought and read my stories.

In this book I have tried to draw on my knowledge of cats, gained from observing these marvellous creatures since our family first acquired one (or perhaps the other way round!) when I was a small child. Of course, readers can decide how much the book is about cats, and how much about people. Maybe it's about both…

I hope very much that there will be at least one sequel to this book, and possibly a children's version, with illustrations. It all depends on agent/publisher interest really.

Needless to say, all agents, publishers and readers can contact me here: acatcalleddog@hotmail.co.uk or via the publishers, or on Twitter: @ACatCalledDog

http://www.troubador.co.uk/book_info.asp?bookid=2177

Cover based on a design by the author ©

BY THE SAME AUTHOR
(writing as PJ Vanston)

Novel

Crump (2010)

Published Short stories

The Last Shark [1]
@Death [2]
The Prague Violin [3]
Mother's Little Helper [4]

1   Published in Shark Focus www.sharktrust.org 2011
2   Published in Pop Cult Magazine issue 12
    www.popcultmag.wordpress.com 2011
3   Winner, second prize, British Czech and Slovak Association com-
    petition 2012 www.bcsa.co.uk. First prize, Global Short Story
    Competition, February 2013.
4   Published 2013. Writing Magazine.

For all the cats…

Tippy,
Podge and Nana,
Hobbes,
Max and Leo,
Fifi and Frodo,
Honey and Bumble

…and all the cats to come.

CHAPTER 1

Cats are not dogs. And dogs are not cats. Even two-legs know that.

But Dog was a cat, because that was his name: he was a cat – a cat called Dog – and he was happy with that too.

But to call him a cat was not entirely accurate either, because he sometimes felt like a kitten, more than a cat – or perhaps he was just somewhere in between? He wasn't sure really.

All he knew was that he had seen just one summer, which made him older than a kitten but younger than a full-grown cat, so perhaps he was more a *kitten-cat* than anything else.

Dog was a most handsome cat, with a black-and-white coat of thick glossy fur. His black pointy ears twitched like whiskers at the slightest of sounds, and the whiskers either side of his cold wet nose twitched like ears sometimes too. Wide bright eyes peered out from the middle of his round face which was, like his chest, mostly white. There were black patches here and there, like paw prints, and one of these circled his right eye, and covered the top half of his head.

At the other end, he had a tail – just the one – which was long and black but for a little white tip, like a magician's wand: it looked for all the world as if he'd accidentally dipped the end of it in a pot of white paint. This he wagged whenever he was happy or excited, which was not at all what you'd expect from a cat. In fact, it was more what you'd expect from a dog – which was, as it happens, why his name was 'Dog' in the first place.

One day, Dog was walking along a garden wall when he came face to face with a big ginger tomcat, with a huge terrifying face, and huge terrifying eyes to match his huge terrifying teeth. The monster screamed at him.

'Miiiiiaaaaaooooowwwwww!' it said, in no uncertain terms, 'Yeeeeeoooooowww!'

Dog watched the tom's performance, wondering what to do. Maybe he too should puff himself up to be as big and tall as he could, forcing his fur to stand on end like a caterpillar's? Then he could try and emit the loudest and most hideous noisy noise too, just like the ginger tom?

Dog understood this cat's behaviour and had seen it many times before. He knew that this tom was only guarding his wall – one that Dog had never walked along before, but not unlike those he used to walk along at home – a wall which he knew was definitely not his at all. Actually, it was a wall that was nowhere near his old territory, because the kitten-cat really was a very long way from home indeed.

The ginger monster miaowed and screamed again, louder this time, hissing and spitting with as much sound and fury as he could muster. But still the little black-and-white kitten-cat stood there wide-eyed on the wall, just looking at him. He didn't run away – in fact, he didn't even flinch! This, thought the ginger tom, required immediate action.

Dog watched as the tom-cat, whose screaming had now become a sort of low growl, raised a paw in the air. This cheered the kitten enormously – even though there were rather a lot of claws showing, he noticed.

'It must mean he's just trying to be friendly,' thought Dog, and he lifted a paw of friendship in return, whilst doing what he always did when he was happy – he wagged his white-tipped tail and yapped.

'Yap yap yap!' said Dog, in a miaow-y kind of way, (though perhaps the sound he made fell somewhere between that of a puppy and a performing seal), swinging and swishing his tail left and right as hard as he could.

Oh, the *horror!*

As if struck dumb by some strange unseen force, the ginger tom-cat fell silent and his face froze into a look of pure feline fear. It was as if all certainty in his world had collapsed into a heap of smouldering rubble at his feet – because, in a way, it had.

'Yap miaow yap yap yap WOOF!' said Dog, bouncing on his paws like a puppy.

Woof?!

WOOF?!!!

A cat saying 'yap yap yap' and WOOF?

And wagging its tail when it's happy!!!!!

The ginger tom had certainly never *ever* seen or heard anything as terrible, as awful, as *wrong* as this before. The kitten-cat before him was behaving, it had to be said, for all the world – and it shamed him to say it – like a *dog!*

Now uncertain and nervous, the ginger cat's eyes and face no longer looked huge and terrifying, but tiny and terrified – and very, *very* confused. He recoiled in horror, and started to walk backwards – slowly, carefully, as cats always must when moving in this fundamentally unnatural direction – hoping that this invader of his garden wall would leave.

This was not a retreat, of course – it was a strategy. A cat needed time to think about such things, needed to sleep on it – and something this strange and disturbing needed several long sleeps, and probably a good few naps too.

If he walked backwards, he would soon reach the end of the wall. Then he would be able to jump down into the garden by the back door and nonchalantly amble towards the cat flap, through which he would squeeze on his way into the kitchen.

He had to defend his home! That was his mission! He was prepared to share his wall, and that had always been his intention. After all, it was only a wall – only a border of his territory. They could call the events on the garden wall a draw, if any other cat happened to ask.

This was the ginger tom's plan anyway. But what he did not expect was the sight – the horrific, dread sight – of this little black-and-white kitten-cat, tail a-wag, ears a-prick – walking towards him – *following him!* – as he walked backwards along the wall, yapping and woofing and barking at him like some horrible, terrifying mutant cat-dog monster thing!

Dog watched as the tom walked backwards away from him along the wall – a tricky manoeuvre for a cat, he knew, and one demanding admiration. He looked friendlier now, so this – Dog thought – must be his way of inviting a fellow feline into his garden.

Dog was absolutely delighted. What luck! He was so pleased to have stumbled into such friendly territory because there are, as all cats know, gardens out there which are not friendly – not friendly at all.

As he walked backwards, the ginger tom saw before him the black-and-white kitten-cat walking towards him ever more quickly, onwards and onwards, a terrible vicious cat-dog monster, yapping and woofing towards him, faster and faster and faster!

So the ginger tom moved faster too, only he was walking backwards, not forwards – and forwards is, as all cats know, the best direction by far.

Now, the ginger tom cat knew this wall. He knew every mossy brick of it. He had walked on it, jumped on it, sat on it, dozed on it, purred on it, washed on it, seen everything-he-wanted-to-see-from-the-corners-of-his-big-yellow-eyes on it. He had stared at the moon and the stars and the clouds and the sky from it on almost every single night of his life – (except that time when he went to *that* place – the 'place of smells and pain' – where the two-legs dressed in white poked him in the most undignified manner in places you would *not* believe!)

But – and it was a very big *but* – he knew the wall *forwards* – whiskers first. Not *backwards* – whiskers last – which was not the same thing at all. And then, the inevitable…

'Miiiiiaaaaaoooooowwwww!' he squealed as he fell, landing with something that any passing two-legs might well have called a thud. He ended up slap bang in the middle of a flowerbed which, happily, was cushioned with the soft green bedding of some pretty nasturtiums with red and yellow flowers.

Now, cats always fall on their feet – even two-legs know that. It is the way it is, the way it was, the way it ever shall be. It is *The Rule*.

However, rules can occasionally get broken in the most extraordinary circumstances – and the circumstances today were, without a doubt, most extraordinary indeed.

The ginger tom got to his paws quickly – or as quickly as he could, (though it was a bit of a struggle, what with his healthily full figure). And when he did so he came face to face with the horrible doggy yappy woofy kitten-cat monster thing who was now right there, in his own garden, staring straight back at him!

The old tom gave himself a much-needed lick.

'Are you… alright?' said Dog, tongue poking out of his little mouth in a concerned manner – which looked, it has to be said, perversely puppy-like.

The old tom stared back at the kitten-cat before him. The creature now seemed to be speaking Cat, not Dog – and he did seem as friendly and elegant as a feline, despite the doggy mannerisms. It was all most strange, and very, *very* tiring.

'Of course I'm alright!' he snapped.

His ribs were aching as much as his sagging tail, but perhaps ever so slightly less than his pride.

'I'm Dog,' said Dog, getting introductions over.

The ginger tom's ears, which were also sagging limp, as though they'd fallen asleep, twitched stiff at this. He really didn't know what to make of a cat called Dog.

Imagine: a cat actually called Dog whose behaviour was sometimes distinctly canine. It wasn't normal or natural at all. Indeed, it was the very stuff of nightmares – for cats, anyway.

It was an insult to feline pride – an unnatural aberration that would surely shame every cat and heap humiliation and disgrace onto the collective head of the species.

Added to that, it was just plain *weird*.

Then, almost before the ginger tom knew what he was doing, he said:

'My name is George,' before adding, 'and this is my garden.'

Just in case there was any misunderstanding.

CHAPTER 2

'I'm sorry to be walking into your garden without asking,' said Dog, 'it's just… I haven't got anywhere else to go, and I was just passing through.'

George looked at Dog, and especially at his wagging tail which, even two-legs know, is usually the signal for unhappiness in a cat.

'Could you stop doing that, please?' said George, rather disturbed at the sight.

Dog followed George's gaze along his body to his white-tipped tail, and through enormous effort stopped it wagging. George nodded in approval.

Just then, a scruffy-looking one-eyed cat with long black-and-grey fur appeared on the garden wall. His name was Eric and he was the local stray.

'Cor blimey!' he said, 'We got a right one 'ere! What's your name, kitten-cat?'

'Dog!' said Dog.

'Where?!' said Eric, looking left and right and left again in panic, turning round to see behind him then in front of him then behind him again, then under and between his legs, until he felt so dizzy that he had to sit down on the wall for a well-earned rest.

George shook his big ginger head at Eric's confusion.

'No no no,' he said, 'it seems that *Dog* is the kitten-cat's name.'

Eric's ears pricked up as his brain tried to take in the enormity of this new and incredible information.

He looked at Dog, then back at George, then back at Dog.

And then he burst out laughing, rubbing his tummy on the top of the wall, taking care to stick his claws into the brickwork first to ensure he wouldn't lose his balance.

'A cat called Dog?' said Eric, 'You're 'avin' a laugh!'

George shook his head: he was not, sad to say, 'having a laugh'. Quite the opposite: he was 'having a frown' (as much as cats can) and indeed could not have been more serious.

Dog wagged his tail happily at Eric – it was always good to make a new friend, and this was his second of the day!

Eric saw Dog's waggly tail and laughed even louder. Dog was delighted that his new friend was so happy, so he joined in, laughing in his own unique way, which was, it has to be said, rather doggish.

'Yap yap yap!' giggled Dog, 'Yappety-yappy-yap!'

George put a paw over his eyes. He was starting to get a headache. Not a hunger headache, but the kind a cat gets when he hears a cat behaving like a dog – which is, it has to be said, a very rare headache indeed. He wished he could put two other paws over his two ears, but that would only leave him with one paw – and it is an undeniable fact that a cat cannot stand on one paw. Those who have tried have failed. Badly.

'Rrrruff!' said Dog, wagging his tail, 'Rrrruff-ruff-ruff!'

By now, Eric was now laughing so hard, guffawing and howling so much, that he wobbled, overbalanced and toppled off the wall into George's garden. He landed solidly on all four paws, then gave himself a little lick to make sure everything was as it should be – and to let every cat know that he had actually intended to jump off the wall all along, albeit in an unusual manner.

'Kitten-cat, *purrrrlease!*' miaowed George.

Dog stopping barking immediately. He even stopped wagging his tail, even though he was still very happy: today was turning out to be a good day, all in all, and he was meeting lots of new friends. He had to try not to get over-excited, but it was such a long time since he'd talked to anyone so friendly that he just couldn't help himself.

'Cor blimey,' said Eric, 'I ain't never seen nuffink like this! A cat what sounds like a dog – a feline fing what wags his tail, not when he's angry, but *when he's 'appy!*'

'It is, one has to say, most unfortunate and highly unusual.'

'It's a bleeding joke, mate, that's what it is. An absolute shocker!'

George could only agree. But what could be done? How could the kitten-cat who had arrived in the garden that day be made to see the error of his ways?

Why was a cat behaving so like a puppy dog anyway? What did it all mean?

Moreover – and this question was preying on George's mind at that troubled hour: *Whither cats?* As a species – and a superior one at that? It was all such a worry.

'You know what, George?' said Eric, 'You should learn 'im!'

'I beg your pardon!' miaowed the old tom, 'What on earth are you talking about?'

'Yeah! You should *learn* the kitten 'ow he can be an 'undred per cent full-on feline cat, innit?'

'Are you suggesting that I actually undertake to *teach* this kitten-cat myself?'

'Like what I said – you's got a *heducation*, George, so it's you what's the best cat round 'ere to learn 'im stuff, like.'

'Oh don't be so ridiculous!' snapped George, 'The kitten-cat's far too old for such a thing.'

'Old? The kit's one summer, at most – an' one summer ain't old, George. I bet life's learnt you loads since you was that age.'

'That's not the point.'

'Oh, ain't it?'

'No, it *isn't*, Eric. I have never ever in all my cat days and nights behaved like a… well… like another species.'

Dog poked his tongue out in confusion at all this: he was, as far as he was concerned, just behaving naturally.

'It'll never work,' said George, and ambled off towards the shed to prepare for a very necessary nap.

He knew that whatever terrible damage had been done to the kitten-cat in his early life was, most probably, permanent. One summer old was a lot, in cat terms, and kittens had to learn the basics in the first days and nights of life – otherwise, George was sad to say, they never really grew up to be the best of cats. This, he knew, was the root cause of much suffering, and such a story of neglect in kitten-hood could be told by many a stray.

'You's just a scaredy-cat,' said Eric.

'I most certainly am not,' miaowed George, knowing full well the stray's tendency to provoke, and trying therefore not to *pounce on the mouse*, 'I just know that it can't be done – it's too difficult. Besides, I am not a teacher – I have never taught any kitten anything before. Moreover, I'm a rather mature cat these days… '

'*Old,* you mean?' miaowed Eric, with a wink.

'A *mature* cat,' reiterated George, 'of advancing years. I need my rest and recuperation in order to perform my duties as a house cat to my usual high standards. I do not have the time – or inclination – to start teaching strays at my time of life. Now that's my final miaow on the matter.'

George looked over to Eric, and then at the kitten.

'Good luck, kitten-cat,' he added, before half-closing his eyes to the world.

Dog wasn't sure what to say. Was he doing something wrong? Behaving badly in some way? Had he offended? He had no idea, so did what he always did when he was confused, and poked his little pink tongue out at the world, in a manner that George may well have called 'puppy-esque'.

'Do you live near here, Eric?' he asked, wondering.

'Oh yeah, kitten,' said the stray with a cheeky grin, 'I does – I lives right here.'

Dog looked puzzled: he thought this was George's garden.

'What he means to say is that he lives everywhere,' yawned George, weary after all the morning's disruption, 'and nowhere.'

Dog looked even more puzzled. How can a cat live everywhere and nowhere at the same time?

He had though heard of cats who lived in two houses with two sets of two-legs, each of whom was unaware of the other, which was an effective, if a little sneaky, way

12

of doubling rations – (cats who indulged in this trick were sometimes referred to ominously in the cat community as *'missing, presumed fed'*).

Eric laughed and rolled over again, giving his paw a little lick of satisfaction. It always seemed to George that his standard of grooming left a lot to be desired. His long-haired fur coat really was disgracefully matted and dirty and of quite shameful appearance for a feline.

'He's a stray,' said George to Dog, embarrassed on Eric's behalf, 'which means that he has no home at all, and no two-legs to look after either.'

Eric squeaked a happy miaow. Dog knew that *he* didn't have a home or two-legs to look after either, but said nothing.

'And a good thing too!' said Eric, 'Two-legs are fine as far as they go, an' they does give yer grub, it's true – but it ain't no one-way street. Oh no… You gotta look after 'em too, be there for 'em, rub up against 'em, be their *slave*… '

'No you do *not!*' snapped George, 'Don't listen to him, kitten-cat!'

George got to his feet. He was angry now – as was evident from the way the ends of his ears were trembling like leaves in the wind. Eric had seen this many times before, and so he knew it would not lead to anything more, such as violence and cat-scratching – not with old George.

'A cat with a two-legs to look after is *never* a slave! On the contrary, he is a cat with a purpose who is made complete by his privileged position in life. He chooses to accept his role, through dignified choice and preference, as is his duty.'

Dog nodded. He didn't want to cause any arguments.

He just wanted to learn as much as he could from these two older and wiser cats – and he seemed to be learning quite a lot today already, which was a good start.

'Each cat to his own,' said Eric, yawning a big yawn, as he always did at that time of day, and at quite a few other times too, 'You'll learn, little kitten-cat, you'll learn – especially if some cat learns you, like.'

George knew Eric had done it on purpose – wound him up by criticising two-legs, thereby ruining his nap. There was nothing else for it – he would have to find a more peaceful place to sleep, away from the din and chaos of what was, he didn't need to be reminded, his own garden! But he was too tired to argue – he just wanted to sleep.

'Sorry, kitten-cat, but I need my nap. I am sure Eric here will be able to teach you a great deal about the joys of being a stray.'

Eric rolled over and laughed. Dog, with tongue poking out in confusion, stood watching George stroll away – (rather arthritically, it has to be said) – in the direction of the neighbour's wall and garden.

'Best fing you can do, kitten, is get some kip – you can grab yourself some grub later, if George lets yer, like.'

Fair enough, thought Dog. How could he expect a cat of George's age to devote any time to teaching him how to be a cat anyway – especially if the task was as hopeless as it sounded?

He would do as Eric said – take a nap, have a feed (if permitted), and then move on.

It seemed that Dog's future would be to live the life of a stray – albeit one who behaved in a most peculiar doggy fashion. But if that was his cat destiny, then there was nothing he could do about it.

It could, after all, be worse: he could actually *be* a dog – though that really didn't bear thinking about.

Dog curled up in the flowerbed next to Eric, closed his eyes and dozed off.

Meanwhile, George was on the verge of drifting off to sleep too. He was curled up under a shrub in the next-door garden – a most delightfully dark and tranquil spot – and greatly looking forward to a refreshing and dreamy sleep.

And then it happened: a bird high up in the tree tweeted.

It wasn't an unusual tweet – and wasn't particularly loud or distinctive either. In fact, it was just a tweet like a million others heard every day. But it was a tweet that mattered.

'Tweet', it went. Just like that.

And then the strangest thing happened to George: he remembered.

Memories rose in his mind like bubbles from the deep and took him back to a time when, as a very young kitten, he had been new to his home. And he remembered how, one day, he had tried to climb the very tree in whose shadow he now reclined.

Now, in those days – and it was a very long time ago – there lived an old black cat next door, a wise old tom who had seen many summers with his fading eyes. This fellow feline had, in a spirit of selfless fellow feline generosity, taken it on himself to teach a clumsy kitten called George all about how to climb that tree – and more importantly, how to get down again and so not get stuck.

And the old tom had taught him so much else besides – about eating and washing and, well, everything really. He had been a real mentor to George when he was growing up, a surrogate father tom to show him the ways of the world and how he too could one day become a successful and effective cat.

That old black tom was long gone now, but in his former student – his protégé – he lived on forever. The knowledge he had passed on to the kitten, the attitudes and aptitudes he had inculcated in his charge, had without a doubt helped his student become a noble and dignified cat. For George was – as all cats who knew him would agree – a most marvellous and magnificent cat, and a real credit to the species.

How long ago that all was! How far away were the carefree days of kitten-hood! Though it all felt like yesterday, of course, as happy memories often do.

But oh, how quickly the time had passed!

How short is the life of a cat! How noble, how dignified, how elegant – but oh, how very short!

The lessons of that old black tom who, despite his age and failing eyesight, gave so much to a kitten in need, had made George the tom he was today. How fondly and well he remembered it all…

And a bird tweeted up in the tree, just as it used to all those many moons ago.

George stood up, his stiff legs creaking their age as he limped out from under the shrub. He leant his head back as far as it would go and gazed up at the tree.

'Tweet tweet tweet,' went the bird, sounding perhaps a teeny bit worried about the little lion of a cat below.

And George knew exactly what he had to do.

Did it matter if this little kitten-cat called Dog went through life behaving – with all the tail-wagging, yappety-yapping and tongue-poking – for all the world like a puppy dog?

Two-legs would probably say 'no' – but then, how would they know the importance of such things?

Did it matter to cats that such a creature – such an aberration – existed in the universe?

Of course it mattered! It mattered more than miaows could say.

The pride of cats was at stake – and the shame of an entire species (the most noble one, too) would be the consequence of inaction and negligence in this matter.

George now recognised this, instinctively and absolutely. And he knew that the selfish decision of an old ginger tom cat to choose peace and quiet over his duty had to be reversed, whether or not his plan worked, whatever the cost may be.

There was nothing else for it. *Something had to be done!*

'By my paws,' mumbled George, remembering – just *remembering* – and he made his way back to his own garden.

'I have an announcement to make,' he miaowed on his return, loud enough to wake Eric and to make the birds in the neighbour's tree tweet just a little louder.

Dog had not been sleeping – merely resting his eyes – and he now opened them to see the old ginger tom sitting before him, watching him closely. The kitten stood up.

Had he done something wrong? Was he in trouble? Maybe George was going to ask him to leave his garden? He looked very serious, anyway. 'Stiff-whiskered' was the word.

'Eric, you are right,' George said, head bowed.

'Cor blimey, guv'nor, that's a first. Are you ill?'

'Shhh, stray. Be quiet. I would like you both to know that I have come to a decision. For reasons which need not concern you, I have changed my mind.'

'Bring out the biscuits!' cheered the stray in celebration.

'My decision does not affect you, Eric – but it does, most significantly, affect the kitten-cat here.'

'Who, me?' said Dog, tongue poking out.

'I fink so,' whispered Eric, 'I's a bit old for a kitten… '

'I have decided, after much considered contemplation, to take it on myself to teach this unfortunate creature, whose upbringing clearly left a lot to be desired, how to be a proper cat.'

'Bloomin' 'eck!' said Eric.

'Really?' said Dog, his white-tipped tail waggling like a wand.

'Indeed,' said George, 'because this is the only way. It will not be easy. It will not be quick. And the chances of failure are high. But it is every cat's duty to help a kitten in need, and this I shall do willingly by providing you with a fine feline education to the best of my ability.'

'But you said before that it wouldn't work,' miaowed Eric.

'I know, and I apologise.'

George bowed his head to Dog.

'The fact is that I do not know if it will work. The kitten-cat is older than the average young learner, and much damage has been done, so we may indeed fail in our quest. But we *must try*. We must believe that success is within our paws' grasp! We must *believe.*'

'*Believe,*' echoed Dog, because it seemed like the best thing to say, somehow – the miaow just sounded good, and right, too.

'A cat must behave like a cat, not like a dog – it is the way things are. And the way to achieve a change, and to help this kitten become a cat, is education.'

'Being un-*heducated* never done me no 'arm,' muttered Eric.

'That's a matter of opinion,' said George – rather cattily, Dog thought.

'I mean, look at me now – well fed, 'appy, fancy free – rollin' in it, I am,' and with that Eric rolled over on the garden path and stretched his body to its full length, making sure every cat present could see his well fed stomach – something George considered vulgar in the extreme.

Eric, George knew, was a bad influence. He'd have to make sure Dog was steered away from cats such as him – strays, lower orders, undesirables, ruffians and wrong 'uns. Though, as strays went, Eric was of a better sort, it had to be said. He could have been passably respectable if he'd tried, which is what made it all so doubly disappointing.

George looked at the kitten-cat:

'So, kitten, what do you say to your pursuing a course of study that will, with hard work, dedication and perhaps just a little luck, transform you from… well… from how you are now, into a proud and noble cat? Do you *believe* you can change, and do you want to? Would you like to accept the offer of my tuition? '

Dog stuck his tongue out and thought – but not for very long. This was the best offer any cat had ever made him. In fact, it was the only offer any cat had ever made him. But it was the best too – by far.

'Oh! Yes! I mean… yes yes yes… of course.'

'Splendid!'

'But… are you… sure?'

'As sure as I have ever been about anything, though it won't be easy – oh no – and you, kitten, will have to work very hard indeed.'

'Oh I will, I will – I'll work as hard as I can. Thank you, George,' and he gave his tail a couple of teeny-weeny wags of joy, which his new teacher – thank goodness – failed to notice.

Then, quite suddenly, his tail stopped wagging, he poked out his tongue in confusion and put up a paw.

'A question? Excellent!' said George, 'Ask away, kitten.'

'I was just wondering,' asked Dog, 'Am I a stray?'

'A stray? A *stray*? By my paws!' said George, appalled, 'No you are most certainly *not* a stray. You, kitten-cat, are a student.'

'A *student*?'

'Yes,' said George, 'a student. For you have much to study, kitten, in order to learn how to be a highly successful and dignified cat.'

By now, Eric was laughing so much that he rolled over into a flowerbed, where he got his long fur all sticky by rolling on a worm.

'Me – a student!' said Dog, waggling his tail and yapping like a puppy as he ran round in circles at the news.

He was so happy and excited that he just couldn't help it, even though George gave him a very hard stare indeed.

CHAPTER 3

'Right,' miaowed George, 'Lesson one. Now pay attention, please, kitten-cat.'

Dog sat up straight and tried not to wag his tail, even though he was ever so excited.

He was now officially a student – and was doing something called *studying* – though Dog didn't feel any different to a few moments before when he wasn't a student really. No doubt he would be able to study precisely why that was the case later on, when he had an education.

For now, though, he had to concentrate on learning how to be a cat. There was, he sensed, a great deal to learn.

George looked thoughtful, cleared his throat with a little authoritative cough, and took a long deep breath.

'As every cat knows,' he began, 'there are a great many aspects to feline life, but the three most important for a cat's wellbeing – the Holy Trinity, if you will – are eating, sleeping and washing. Now, for purposes of convenience, I am not including issues to do with two-legs here as yet – these will be addressed later in the course of study.'

Dog nodded. He was keen to learn all about two-legs

as soon as possible, but was happy to follow the syllabus that George had decided upon: he was, after all, a very old and wise cat, and Dog was a very young and un-wise cat who had rather a lot to learn.

'Of these three,' continued George, 'it is the latter which is arguably the most important – because if you don't get the hygiene right with adequate washing, then eating and sleeping can be exceedingly uncomfortable and just downright unpleasant.'

A look of distaste crept over George's face, as if he'd smelt something disgustingly dirty – or perhaps remembered something even worse.

'A clean cat is a healthy and happy cat,' he said, 'Repeat after me, Kitten… '

'A clean cat is a healthy and happy cat,' said Dog – and so did Eric, who was sitting in the flowerbed watching the lesson from behind some pretty red and yellow nasturtiums.

Eric lifted up a paw and scratched his ear. George glared at him – hard.

'Now look here, stray,' he said, 'this lesson is not for you – though goodness knows you could do with it – so can I ask you please not to create a disturbance? The kitten-cat's education depends on it, you know. Remember, too, that this is *my* garden, and not yours.'

Eric knew George was right. He appreciated the way that George let him use his garden, and his wall, and also let him occasionally eat food from his bowl if he had any spare – which was most of the time, because he was always given so much. Not every cat would be so generous and tolerant. So he wasn't a bad old ginger tom, all things considered.

'Fair enough,' said Eric – he almost said *'fur enough'*

but, knowing how much George hated jokes, didn't want to push it.

'I am trying,' said George, 'to give this little kitten-cat – an unfortunate creature who wags his tail when he is happy, who pokes his tongue out puppy-fashion, and who says *yap*, *woof*, and goodness knows what else – a good education. This is a serious matter and a most urgent priority.'

'I ain't never 'ad no *heducation*,' said Eric, mournfully.

'So you said. Congratulations!' snapped George, 'Now come on, kitten-cat – we shall proceed with the lesson and ignore the stray.'

'But I's quite partial to 'avin one too, if one's available, like… ' said Eric with a long and plaintive miaow.

He was serious: George could see in the single eye staring back from his furry face that he was serious. He also knew, from the smell – (of the dark moist mouldy corners of dustbins that Eric carried around with him like a cloud) – that a lesson or two in cleanliness wouldn't go amiss either.

'Can he stay?' asked Dog, 'Please.'

George considered the innocent fluffy face of the little kitten-cat who had appeared – like the son he had never had – on his garden wall earlier that morning. Then he looked at the scruffy one-eyed old stray called Eric, a cat who had probably never had a home or a two-legs to look after – a cat who had almost certainly never had much contact with respectable felines when a kitten, and who had thus picked up all sorts of bad habits from what George was wont to call, 'the wrong sort of cat'.

'Oh go on, George,' said Eric, 'I won't be no nuisance – promise!'

'Pleeease,' said Dog, and then he gave a little plaintive miaow as all kitten-cats should in times like these. Nobody had shown him how to do this: he just knew somehow, and instinctively felt that it was what he should do in the circumstances.

George sighed a weary old tom sigh of strained yet selfless tolerance.

'Oh, alright,' came a grumpy miaow of permission. Eric and Dog bounced up and down on their paws in excitement, 'But on one condition...'

'Anyfink you ask,' said Eric, 'your wish is my command, guv'nor!' and with that he rolled right over, getting his fur even more sticky with the worm that now lay in the flowerbed, still stunned and squashed by its earlier encounter.

'Would you stop doing that?!'

Eric was baffled – all he had done was roll over, as all cats do from time to time.

'Doing what? I ain't done nuffink!'

'Flattening all The Lady's flowers... Quite apart from anything else, a cat never knows what he's going to pick up when doing such things. I mean, look at that – a worm.'

Dog leaned forward to see a long sticky worm stuck in the stray's matted fur. Eric bent his neck to have a look too, taking a good look close-up with his left eye (the one that still worked). Then with one well-practised and delicate motion of his tongue, he lifted the worm off his skin and manoeuvred it into his mouth where, after a couple of crunchy chews, it began its final slippery journey down into his stomach.

George looked at Eric with an expression somewhere between dismay and fulfilled expectation.

Dog wondered when he would have a lesson about how to do things like that – he was sure that were lots of worms around to practise on.

'Well… ' said the stray, chewing, 'S'all protein, innit?'

'Now look, Eric, please. No rolling over in The Lady's flowerbeds – is that clear?'

'Clear as sky water, guv'nor. Is that the one condition?'

'It most certainly is not… and can you stop calling me that too?'

'What? – *'guv'nor'*? – guv'nor?'

'You sound like the worst sort of alley cat. It lowers the tone. From now on, you should call me George at all times.'

'Lucky it's your name then, innit?'

George said nothing. Dog gave Eric a hard stare – he wanted to get on with the lesson and the stray was now wasting time mucking about.

'George it is then,' said Eric, noticing the kitten's disapproving look, 'Is that the one condition?'

'No it is not,' said George, 'the one condition is that if you are permitted to stay, you should understand and acknowledge that I am the teacher, and you are the student. That is our relationship, and for the duration of all lessons, I shall be unquestionably superior to you and shall thus expect your full attention and deference at all times. There must be discipline!'

'Dissy-plinn,' nodded Eric.

'Discipline,' nodded Dog.

'Discipline,' said George, 'because without discipline there is chaos, anarchy, disorder – and unclean cats. You know, I remember a time when… '

Dog put his paw up.

'Yes, kitten-cat,' said George.

'Sorry to interrupt… but… I mean… can we start *learning* something now please?'

George had got so caught up in sharing his views on discipline that he had quite forgotten he was supposed to be giving a lesson. He was meant to be in the process of teaching the kitten-cat about how to wash, he remembered – and wouldn't have forgotten if that ill-mannered stray Eric hadn't interrupted either, so it was absolutely clear where the blame for his forgetfulness lay.

'Splendid!' announced George, 'Well done, kitten-cat. I was wondering how long it would take you to notice that.'

Eric was going to say something but decided against it. Instead, he scratched his ear, into which some little creature was crawling, probably on the way to meet his friends who were already in there wriggling and tickling about.

'Really, Eric,' tutted George, 'you can be so disgracefully lackadaisical at times.'

'Lacky-wot-sical?'

'Oh never mind. Right, where was I? Ah yes… Lesson one… ' George cleared his throat. 'Washing for cats. Now there are many types of washing for many types of situations. There is, for example, the morning wash and the *post-prandial* clean-up… '

'The *what?*' said Eric, baffled.

'It means the *after-meal* clean-up.'

'Well why didn't yer just say so?' said the stray, winking his good eye at Dog, who was certainly glad Eric had asked, because he didn't know what it meant either.

'Now, it is essential to know the difference between the wash for hygiene and the wash for effect. The latter is arguably as important as the former. You can, for example, use a wash to change the subject, to hide embarrassment, to call attention to yourself or just to generally enhance the feeling you wish to convey to your two-legs. Needless to say, the stance taken when having your wash for effect must be given some serious thought. The pose should be elegant, the manner one of calculated confidence, thus… '

George sat up, turned his head slightly and gave his shoulder a couple of little licks. His face was completely focused on the task, and bore an expression of aloof insouciance when he had finished.

'See?' said George, 'Now you try, kitten.'

Dog emulated the sitting-up pose and gave his shoulder a few little licks, with what he hoped was a look of deep concentration on his face.

'That's simply splendid, kitten-cat. Well done!' said George.

'Nice one, kitten!' said Eric.

Dog gave his magician's wand of a tail the merest flicker of a wag. He was so excited to be learning something that he just couldn't help himself.

Today was turning out to be magic indeed!

CHAPTER 4

'Sacrebleu!' said the tabby cat, peering through the hedge into George's garden, 'Incroyable!'

Usually, when he walked along the wall here on ordinary days he would just see George, the old fat tom he'd known for so many summers, sitting on his wall or lying in the garden. More often than not, he would be sleeping – which was understandable, because he did have to guard a whole long wall and garden all by himself, which was no doubt very tiring indeed.

Today, however, was no ordinary day. For what the tabby saw when he looked through the hedge was none other than three cats – George, Eric the stray, and a new little kitten-cat he had never seen before – sitting in the garden with their back legs raised like flagpoles, washing (if he wasn't mistaken) in unison. Their washing could even have been called *synchronised*, as though someone had ordered them to perform in this way.

This was most strange and un-cat-like, he thought – most strange and un-cat-like indeed.

The tabby crept silently along the wall and hid behind a buddleia bush at the end of the neighbour's garden – he would get a better view from here of the horrors taking place below.

'That's much better, kitten-cat,' George said, 'but you must try to lift your hind leg a bit higher in order to facilitate the most efficient washing of the nether regions.'

Dog stretched his back paw up as far as he could – without overbalancing and falling over.

'Like this?' he said.

'That's splendid, kitten-cat. And don't forget, you'll get better with practice. Keep it up now! No flagging!'

'Cor blimey,' said Eric, 'I can't stretch no further, George – I's already feelin' muscles I never *knewed* I had – I'll do meself an injury, I will! I ain't one o' them *Hindian* yoga cats, y'know!'

'You can be assured, Eric, that no cat ever did themselves an injury whilst washing.'

'Not unless they fell off a wall when doing it, eh, George?' said Eric, the bright memory of that morning's events twinkling in his eye.

'Never mind all that. Right, let's try it again,' said George, clearing his throat with a convenient cough, 'Take your sitting positions. Ready?'

'Ready,' said Dog.

'As I'll ever be!' said Eric.

'Now just follow what I do. And… *Sit* two three four, *leg* two three four, *lean forward* two three four – and tongues ready – *lick* two three four, *lick* two three four, *lick* two three… '

'Zut alors!' exclaimed a voice – one which, when George heard it, almost made his considerable (though well-proportioned) frame overbalance in shock and slump inelegantly on the garden path.

'Well done, kitten-cat,' said George, straightening himself up and giving his paw a lick, 'We'll continue with this later. Remember to practise several times a day, both after and before every meal and nap as an absolute minimum. Is that clear?'

'Oh yes,' said Dog, 'clear…as sky water,' and with that the kitten leapt to his feet and wagged his tail in happiness.

George pretended not to see this aberration. He was simply too tired to correct the kitten-cat – after so much effort and exertion, he badly needed a lie down, though that would have to wait now that a guest was here.

'François!' exclaimed Eric, 'I ain't seen you for moons and moons, mate!'

'I aff been travelling,' said François, sauntering towards them on the wall, 'far away, over zee 'edge, 'sthru zer fields, into zer woods, into zer place of zer two-legs, out of zer place of zer two-legs, out of zer woods, into zer fields, over zee 'edge – et voilà, 'ere I am. Bonjour mes amis.'

'Good day, François,' said George, who knew him to be a very well-travelled and sophisticated feline of most superior standing, and so was always careful to show the requisite reciprocal respect.

'Allo Georges,' said François, 'and may I to say 'ow 'andsome and 'ealthy you are look, mon ami.'

George almost blushed under his fur – though he knew François's observations to be, as usual, highly perceptive, intelligent and wise.

'But please Georges, can you please to tell to me what ziss eez you do today?'

Eric looked at George; Dog looked at George; George would have looked at George if he could, but instead looked into the sea-green eyes of the lithe and lissom tabby cat above him on the wall.

'Indeed I can,' said George, knowing that an explanation was due, 'Today, I have been giving a lesson to these cats – Eric, you know, and a new kitten called…'

'Dog!' yapped Dog, wagging his tail at this new exotic visitor. But François did not really notice him – he was more worried about the dog.

'Où est le chien? Where he is?' said François, nervously looking left and right and up and down and left and right again, but seeing no dog of any description anywhere.

George did wish Dog would stop saying his name like that – if only to spare his nerves, let alone those of any other cat who heard him say it.

'Ah no, you see, a common mistake,' said George, 'What this little kitten-cat means is that his name is… unfortunately…'

'Dog!' said Dog, wagging his tail cheerily: it was a name George found hard to say, for obvious reasons.

'Quite,' said George, wanting at that precise moment to bury his face in his paws forever, but knowing he couldn't. His dignity and status would just have to survive the scrutiny of the sophisticated and well-travelled François.

'Straight up,' butted in Eric, 'This 'ere's a cat called Dog, if you can believe it!'

'Sacrebleu!' said François, gasping with the shock, 'Zut alors!'

'Oh you ain't heard the 'alf of it, mate. Go on kitten cat, do your doggy noise – barkin' an'… whatever…'

George took a sharp intake of breath in order to tell the kitten-cat that under no circumstances was he to make such awful and annoying unnatural doggy noises, no matter how much any other cat or two-legs or anyone else asked him to. After all, he was not a circus animal but a cat, however confused, and thus his role in life demanded that he act with decorum and dignity at all times.

But he was too late…

'Miiiiiaaaoooowww yap-yap-yap, rrruff-ruff-ruff, yap-yap-yap!' said Dog.

François stood on the wall, sad green eyes surveying the scene, pricked tabby ears twitching this way and that, trying to hear every odd dimension of the strange and disturbing music that filled the air. His delicate jaw hung ever so slightly open in amazement and shock.

Could he believe his ears? Did his eyes deceive him? Was there really before him, in the 'garden of Georges', a kitten-cat bouncing up and down wagging its tail like some pea-brained puppy dog, yapping and yelping and barking and woofing in a way no self-respecting cat could ever countenance?

François had travelled widely. He had seen the sun rise on strange and distant lands where animals behaved in most peculiar fashions. He had eaten exotic strangely-flavoured and spiced foods in the company of cats so diverse and unfamiliar and speaking such strange languages that they were almost of a different species. He had met cats of so many colours and shapes and sizes, some of which looked so unlike cats that it seemed incredible that they were even feline. But they were all – every last weird one of them – even the most exotic and oddly-behaved of them, very definitely and distinctly cats. And they all, but all, made cat noises too – they all spoke Cat. Not Dog, but Cat. That is just the way it is.

But never, not on all of his travels – not even when he watched the sun set golden on the silver southern seas, or crossed the scorching sun-baked deserts of the Orient, or listened to the squawks and growls of animals unknown in the dark distant jungles of the Tropics – had he seen or heard a cat who behaved and sounded just like a dog. Especially one who stuck his tongue out and wagged his tail like a puppy!

'Zut alors!' said François, tutting in dismay, 'Mais c'est dommage. C'est très grave, ça. Je veux dire… I mean to say… Georges – zees eez a pity. One must to call un chat un chat, non?'

George had no idea what François was miaowing on about now – something foreign, obviously. But for some strange reason he knew exactly what the well-travelled tabby meant.

'C'est très sérieux, vraiment – ziss eez zer situation most serious, n'est-ce pas?'

George sighed a deep fur-tingling sigh. He knew that such things could shame a cat, bring disgrace and dishonour on all respectable and dignified felines. But he also knew that it was his duty to take care of such a confused little kitten-cat, to teach him right from wrong, to give him everything that he should have been given when a new-born kitten – to strive to undo the damage done, however daunting the task.

So he would bear his burden willingly and stoically, with honour, with dignity, and with good grace, as was befitting his status as a mature, well-mannered and generally marvellous cat.

What had started as such an ordinary day – a day when he would eat (six times), sleep (three times, plus naps), patrol his wall and do his rounds and inspections thoroughly (twice), and wash (carefully and often) – had become something so strange and peculiar, so out of the ordinary, that George was quite put out, to say the least. And he did not like being put out – he did not like it one little bit.

In one elegant liquid motion, François jumped down from the wall, and came over for a closer look. Dog thought this a very friendly thing to do, so wagged his tail and yapped and barked even more than he was doing already to welcome this new and exotic animal. François was his third friend of the day, which was something of a record and all very exciting! Now he had three friends – which was plenty for a kitten-cat, he thought, and sounded just about the right number too.

Eric rolled in the flowerbed, giggling, glad he was alive – right here, right now – to witness such history in the making. That incident last year with the two-legs' wheel-box had been a close-run thing. And it hadn't been his first scrape either – as the scratches and scars on his body and face, not to mention his always-closed blind right eye, made clear. But he was doubly glad he had survived them all so he could witness this – he wouldn't have missed it for the world.

George sighed deeply. There was no point in hiding the enormity of his predicament – not from an old acquaintance like François.

'I think,' said George, 'that the situation may well be more serious than I at first realised.'

'I sink,' said François, 'zat what you sink, eez also what I sink.'

And they both shook their heads at the seriousness of the situation, as Dog yapped and barked and woofed before them, wagging his tail and poking his pink tongue out at his new-found friends, and feeling happier than he had ever felt before in his whole little life.

CHAPTER 5

It was while George, François and Eric were watching Dog show them his nether regions washing routine, pondering what could be done about the whole unfortunate situation, that a black she-cat called Fifi arrived.

'Ay-up,' said Eric, 'Her Majesty's 'ere.'

'I would ask you not to be so impertinent, stray' said George, straightening his whiskers with a careful wipe of his paw.

'Ahhh,' sighed François, 'Mademoiselle Fifi…'

'*Miss* Fifi, if you please,' said George, 'No need for all that foreign nonsense here.'

'Who's… Miss Fifi?' asked Dog.

'Shhh!' said George – (rather rudely, Dog thought) – 'Such things are *not* for kitten-cats.'

'Specially kitten-cats what finks they is dogs!' chortled Eric.

'Will you please be quiet,' said a worried-looking George, who was busy licking his paw and wiping his face, just to make sure no fur was sticking up (which can happen to even the best of cats if they're not careful).

''Ere,' whispered Eric to Dog, 'I fink somecat's a little bit in love with Miss Fifi.'

Dog pondered for a moment, looked at each cat there one by one, then turned back to Eric who was winking at him with his one good eye.

'But... who?' asked Dog, the pinkness of his tongue poking out in confusion.

Eric purred, rolled on his back and exposed his large well-fed stomach for everyone – especially a she-cat called Fifi – to see.

'You're in love with Fifi, Eric?' asked Dog.

'Me... and 'im... but 'specially 'im,' he said, nodding in George's direction, 'Ain't no-one 'ere who ain't got a soft paw for Miss Fifi – and wouldn't give her a tender tickly bite if he could neither... '

'I always think crudeness is a particularly unattractive quality in a cat, don't you?' snapped George, watching Fifi sashay along the wall for all the world like a princess in the most elegant, the most beautiful, the most delicate way.

George harrumphed:

'But what do you expect from a stray? Miss Fifi knows breeding when she sees it, oh yes... '

'Mademoiselle Fifi!' said François, jumping up on the wall in front of the she-cat in what George thought was a terribly rude and forward manner, 'Enchanté.'

The long, sleek she-cat sauntered casually along the wall, looked up at François, and gave a little chirrup of a purr-miaow. Then she looked down at George – who straightened up immediately to appear as tall as he could – and Eric, rolling in the flowerbed as if quite the worse for wear for catnip.

She also saw a little black-and-white kitten cat she'd never seen before and wondered who he was. Fifi always liked meeting new friends, so long as they treated her with the appropriate respect. It was always useful to get to know all the local toms too, however young – they always got bigger in the end, she knew. And she saw immediately that one more summer would turn this kitten-cat into the handsomest tom in the neighbourhood.

George was just about to say something, to express his views on the wellbeing of the wall, the frequency of sky water, and the growing problem with strays in the local area – which Fifi, from a good home like George, but with several two-legs to look after (how did she do it? Must be a supercat!) would surely be able to appreciate – when Dog beat him to it.

'Dog!' he said, with a very barky sort of miaow.

Miss Fifi suddenly lost all her composure. It was as if someone had cut the invisible puppet-strings supporting her elegant body – and the serene sleekness of her frame became in an instant as jagged as rocks. She looked this way and that, nervous and tense, stretching to see the world from every available angle. Her breathing was fast and hard, and a look of terrified panic was etched in her emerald eyes.

'M... Miss... F... F... Fifi, I... I mean... he... I mean... ' bumbled George.

'Zere eez not zer dog here, Mademoiselle Fifi!' said François, 'Il n'y a pas de chien ici!'

'Miss Fifi,' miaowed the old tom, when he had composed himself, 'please accept my... our... apologies if you were startled... and may I say how healthy and sleek your beautiful black coat is looking this afternoon... '

'Wiz zee eyes who shine like zer stars and zer moon, and zer glossy fur, dark like zer night of passion... '

'Alright alright,' snapped George, 'that's quite enough of that sort of thing, thank you, François.'

Fifi looked calmer now, but not as calm as when she had sashayed along the wall a few moments before. Her heart was still drumming at double-quick speed with the shock of the possible presence of dog, and she was still panting with the effort.

'You see, Miss Fifi, this kitten-cat here is called Dog. That, I am somewhat embarrassed to report, is the poor creature's name.'

'There isn't any *real* dog, Miss Fifi,' piped up the kitten, 'I only said *Dog* because that's my name, not because…'

'Will you *shush up!*' said George with a loud miaow, the tips of his ears trembling with irritation.

Dog's tail stopped wagging and wilted like a comedy magician's wand between his legs. He tried to think about what he was doing wrong, but couldn't think of anything – all he had done was introduce himself.

'Notwithstanding the complexities of the situation, I am pleased to announce that, as the most senior feline, I have been appointed to be the kitten's teacher – his mentor, if you will – and so it falls to me to instruct him in all aspects of how to be a most marvellous and successful cat…'

'Appointed?' scoffed Eric, 'Self-appointed more like.'

'With my great experience of life, and paternal instincts second to none, I feel sure that with the support of all fellow felines, this mission – to turn a confused little kitten into a proper cat – cannot fail to be an enormous success.'

Fifi looked down at Dog.

Dog looked up at Fifi and George.

François and Eric looked up at Fifi too – and so they all saw her reaction when Dog, who just couldn't help himself, then started bouncing up and down on his paws, wagging his tail, and trying to explain to Fifi all about who he was:

'Miiiiiaaaaaoooooowwww yap yap yap woof woof woof!' he said.

The last time such a look of horror had been fixed on Fifi's face was when a two-legs' wheel-box came straight towards her when she was investigating the free food that someone had put right in the middle of the road (a squashed seagull, as it happens). This had taken place the previous year and the she-cat had only just survived the experience, hence the delicate state of her nerves.

Now there was no two-legs' wheel box coming towards her, frightening her to her feline core. And it was not even a dog, either, who was rattling her. Dogs were, at least, a highly recognisable and noisy species – (most of them were just not bright enough to hide silently, as cats do). No, it was another cat – a small black-and-white kitten, who was bouncing up and down like a puppy, yapping and barking at Fifi, and *running towards her*.

That was it – she'd had enough. Fifi turned on her paws and raced off along the wall and into the neighbouring gardens, running as rapidly as her little legs would carry her, homeward bound in a hurry.

'Miss Fifi!' cried George, 'Come back!'

But it was too late. Fifi was gone.

George, whose expression seemed half-way between anger and sadness, glared at Dog. François peered down at the kitten-cat from the wall, and Eric, sprawling on his back in the flower bed, looked up at him.

And Dog didn't know where to look, so he looked at the ground. His tail stopped wagging, his ears unpricked and fell flat against his head, and his little body sank into a square with his paws tucked underneath.

'Sorry,' he said, 'I... '

'The Lady!' said George, and with that he galloped – (well, as much as a rather solid and mature cat *can* gallop) – towards the house. He had heard the key turning in the front door, and within moments was squeezing his way through the cat flap.

'Never mind about Fifi! She'll be back – she's just a little... nervy... tha'sall.'

'She's a very beautiful cat,' chirruped Dog.

'Oh not you an' all,' said Eric, with a snigger as dirty as a dustbin.

'Zer Lady, she eez 'ere maintenant,' explained François, 'Ziss eez what you must to sink about now, mon petit.'

'But,' wondered Dog, 'Who is *The Lady*?'

Eric knew he'd have to take charge of the situation, now George had gone inside.

'D'yous remember how George was bangin' on 'bout every cat needin' a two-legs to look after, like?'

Dog did remember, and said so.

'Well, The Lady is George's two-legs. She means everyfink to the old tom.'

'Ah oui,' said François, 'c'est vrai, ça.'

'More than Miss Fifi?' said Dog.

'Oh yeah – but in a sort of... different, two-legs way,' explained Eric, 'You'll understand when you's older.'

Dog supposed he would, and was so glad he was having lessons to help him learn about things he wouldn't know until he was older too. He knew it would prove useful to know what he didn't know later on – though he didn't know exactly how yet.

But he had to admit that he would have preferred to know a bit more right here and now, had he been given the choice.

CHAPTER 6

George stood in the hall by the front door.

There they were – the legs of his two-legs – the legs he rubbed against every day when The Lady came home to him. Just him. Only him.

He was already purring – loudly, thunderously, magnificently – just so The Lady would be sure to hear him. She would then reach down and stroke his back, as she always did.

Maybe she'd even pick him up and cuddle him, if she didn't have any shopping to carry. But if she did, he would follow her into the kitchen and there she would reward him for his attentiveness with something delicious and tasty, an extra treat before dinner and the main course (or courses, sometimes).

So, as per usual, George walked forward to greet The Lady, tail proudly vertical held high in the air. And, also as per usual, he started pushing up against The Lady's ankles, nudging them tenderly, waiting for the inevitable hands to descend from the heavens and lift him up into that warm and loving embrace – the one that meant that The Lady was happy, that she was his, that all was well with the world.

But that day was different – and not in a good way,

either – because The Lady's legs were not the only two to cross the threshold. They were followed by two more legs – legs covered in clothes – male legs (George could smell them before he saw them).

George did not recognise The Man. He had met all of The Lady's friends who would visit the house, and this was definitely not one of them. No, this two-legs was new and peculiar, and smelt it – in truth, he smelt downright unpleasant. The old tom twitched his nose at the noisome pong.

The Lady reached down to George and patted his head. Then, after closing the front door, she led the stranger into the living room.

George was not used to being ignored in such a rude and vulgar fashion – and the merest pat was tantamount to being ignored when compared to the usual attention he received.

Maybe The Lady was unwell? Maybe she needed George to remind her that, as she was *his* two-legs, this was a matter of some concern to him, and it thus fell to him to comfort her and make her feel better?

Something wasn't right – it was so obvious that even a creature as simple-minded as a puppy would have been able to see it, had one been in the vicinity.

Keen not to miss anything, and in order to closely observe and monitor all events and conversations, George followed The Lady and her visitor into the living room. He watched as The Man sat himself down on the sofa.

'Cup of tea?' asked The Lady.

'Wouldn't say no. Milk two sugars, ta.'

The Lady then left the living room to go into the kitchen. George, considering it his duty to find out everything he could about the intruder, jumped up on the armchair to get a closer look. He had just done so, and was busy inspecting this new two-legs – who smelt even worse close up – when he was grabbed from below by a pair of big cold hands.

'Come on, fat boy!' said The Man, 'Let's have a look at you.'

George had never *ever* been spoken to in such a fashion. This rude, uncouth, ill-behaved male two-legs couldn't possibly be a friend of The Lady's. He must have forced his way in, and was most probably a desperate felon – after all, he had forced her to let him in the house and serve him rations, so who knew what else he was capable of?

'Miiiiiaaaaaooooowwwww!' wailed George, doing his duty to warn The Lady of the imminent danger. He was still in the firm clutches of The Man, but, if needs be, he would be happy to sacrifice himself to allow The Lady to escape. George had lived a good life and so was more than willing to respond to the call of duty, whatever the consequences.

The Lady came first. Always.

'Bit grumpy, isn't he?' said The Man.

'Oh?' called The Lady from the kitchen, 'That's just George. He's friendly really.'

'Bit fat too!' sneered The Man, 'Cor, what a porker!'

There followed a laugh – *a laugh!* – from the kitchen. This, as far as George was concerned, was solid and indisputable evidence of coercion. The Lady would never laugh at him in such a mocking manner of her own volition – *with* him, yes; *at* him, never! Indeed, she had herself often stated to her friends that George was not fat at all, but simply *'in proportion'* – (and those were

44

her very words!) – for a tom-cat of his mature years and well-padded plumpity.

'Too many titbits eh?' said The Man, 'You need to go on a diet, fatso!' – and then he held George up as though he were a prize catch caught in a fishing contest.

And then – *and then!* – something happened that was so awful, so humiliating, so vulgar that something had to be done. With George held up in one hand and a finger extended in the other, The Man jabbed the old tom's now-exposed and rather sensitive stomach with every word he spoke:

'Too... many... titbits... and... too... much... grub... makes... you... a... fat... fat... fat... *fat*... pussycat!!!'

George was stunned. He was being poked in the most sensitive places by someone who had quite obviously forced The Lady to allow him into the house – someone of whose existence he was not aware until a few moments before – and someone who was now jabbing him in his tummy as though he were some sort of common farm animal or zoo exhibit!

It was too much. George was a big supporter of the rule of law, he really was – but at times like these, there was only one thing for it: the rule of *claw*.

With one swift swish of his right paw (claws extended) he scrammed The Man on his forearm and, in one forceful twisting manoeuvre, unshackled himself from the two-legs' grasp. He then dashed out to the kitchen to tell The Lady just how much danger she was in. There was still time for her to escape, if she hurried.

'Yeeeeoooowwww!' yelled The Man, 'The fleabag scrammed me!'

George was by now in the kitchen, telling The Lady everything:

'Miiiiaaaaaooooowww-yeeeooooow ww-yeeeoooooww-wahwow!' he said, in quite clear and specific terms, so there could be no misunderstanding.

'George!' said The Lady, 'You didn't, did you?'

The Man walked into the kitchen and held out his arm. On the bronzed and tautly-muscled skin there were several small beads of dark red blood oozing, like little liquid jewels, from the recently-clawed wound.

George explained everything to The Lady again. She knew he wasn't a fleabag – (it was she who administered the treatment to ensure he was flea-free, after all!) – just as she knew how loyal and loving he was. But The Man had obviously brainwashed her in some devious and underhand way which made her completely unable to understand anything George was saying – that was the only explanation.

'It's fine,' said The Man, 'it's just a scratch.'

And then The Lady ran The Man's forearm under the cold tap, in a manner so close and familiar that George found it all rather disturbing. She patted his skin dry with a towel – (in *just* the same way she patted *him* dry when he came in from the garden sopping wet after he'd been caught in sky water) – and then they both looked down at a very glum and grumpy-looking George.

'I don't know what's got into him; he's usually so… placid… a real old teddy bear… '

And then – *and then* – The Lady did something so awful, so out of character, that George was by now utterly convinced that The Man had brainwashed her. She leant down and gave him a gentle smack on his back.

'Naughty cat,' she said, 'That's no way to treat guests, George!'

46

The Man watched all this with a smug smile of satisfaction on his face: evidence, if more were needed, of his disreputable and evil intentions.

'I'm so sorry,' said The Lady, again (which was way too much apologising – and therefore deeply suspect, George knew).

'Not a problem,' said The Man, lighting a cigarette, 'If he does it again, we'll have him put down eh?'

Silence. George looked at his mistress.

Could she? Would she? Had things gone that far? He may have been a bit stiff of limb lately, a tad plodding of paw, but he had years in him yet – several summers, at least.

And how on earth could The Lady be seriously listening to the opinions of a two-legs who had just stuck a burning 'smoke-stick' into his mouth anyway? Surely that was proof positive, if more were needed, that he was of laughably low intelligence?

'Just joking,' chuckled The Man, 'The look on your face!'

'I've had George for years now,' said The Lady, relieved, 'it wouldn't be the same without him.'

George's chest puffed up with pride. His strategy was working – he was managing to bring The Lady back from the controlling clutches of the interloper. That meant he could now de-brainwash her and make her realise the danger she was in.

'Bit old and fat, though, isn't he? And violent with it!'

'Oh but he's George – he's gentle as a kitten really.'

At last, the old tom was persuading The Lady to see sense, to see that he and she were the only individuals (with two legs or four) who should live in that house. Soon, The Lady would send The Man packing with a flea in his ear – that'd larn him for calling George a fleabag! And they wouldn't see him ever again, not ever, and…

Up George went in The Lady's arms.

Out George went through the opened back door.

Down George went onto the garden path.

'By my paws!' gasped George, 'Miiiiaaaaooooowwww, purrrrup!'

But it was no good – The Lady had obviously become suddenly deaf, probably caused by some evil spell cast by The Man earlier, which the old tom hadn't noticed, what with all the noise and kerfuffle.

'Now, stay out here George, if you can't behave. I'm putting the cover on the cat flap too. A day in the wild won't do you any harm, not in this warm weather.'

And with that, The Lady left him there – him, George, the top cat of the house, the guardian and protector of his two-legs, The Lady's loyal and devoted friend and companion.

'Serves you right, ginger,' called The Man, with the wickedest of smiles on his face.

The back door closed and George heard the cat flap cover being slotted on. There was no way he would be able to get back into the house now – not until The Lady took it off again, anyway.

George sat stunned – and not a little put out – on the garden path. When he turned around he could see Eric's solitary eye blinking at him, François's whiskers drooping sad and forlorn at his predicament, and Dog's little pink tongue poking out as far as it would go in absolute befuddlement.

'Right,' said George, keeping his chin up with considerable exertion, 'Everything is alright and under control. The situation here is quite clear, as I see it, and

I… I shall decide presently on an appropriate course of action.'

'What *app-o-pro-po…* what course of action?' said Eric, not seeing why George had to use such long miaow-words anyway.

Dog and François looked at George. They could tell he was thinking, and thinking hard, by the way his eyes were half-closed and his ears were flickering with twitches on his head.

'You don't expect me to make such an important decision *on the paw*, do you?' he replied, eventually.

Dog and Eric and François shook their heads – they each thought it was the kindest thing to do, in the circumstances.

'Fellow felines, a course of action as crucial as this cannot be undertaken lightly, without due consideration, so we need one thing and one thing only.'

Three blank cat faces looked back at him.

'A plan!' miaowed George, 'We need a plan!'

'Course,' said Eric, 'Just like what I's gonna say. A *plaaan!*'

'But first,' yawned the old tom, 'a nap. A cogitating cat obviously can't be expected to think on a sleep-deprived mind. It's just not natural.'

They all agreed and settled down to sleep, not necessarily knowing what 'cogitating' meant, but knowing that naps have a tendency in cats to produce the most wonderful of ideas…

CHAPTER 7

George stretched his paws awake with an enormous, enjoyable yawn.

It was a beautifully sunny day – a day which needed to be prepared for in the appropriate and traditional fashion. So George decided to go into the kitchen for breakfast, which would give him sufficient energy to patrol his territory with all necessary vim and vigour.

He was on his way there, when something – some deeply-felt instinctive force – made him turn around and head towards the end of the garden. He jumped up onto the wall and sniffed the air. Something strange was going on – something very strange indeed.

With not a little effort, George jumped up onto the wall at the end of the garden. He looked left, down the road (which he never crossed, because of the dangers of two-legs' wheel-boxes); then right, up the lane (which was too narrow for wheel-boxes but which two-legs and felines used regularly); then at the garden of the next-door neighbours' house, with the pond at its centre and its large tall tree.

Silence. No noise at all. Not even birds tweeting to greet the new day, as is their usual habit – (birds not being the most intelligent of creatures, despite their undeniable aerodynamic ability).

Where were the other cats? There were always feline four-paws about if you knew where to look and listen.

But George was completely alone. Eric, François, and the new kitten-cat called Dog, were nowhere to be seen.

Then he heard the rumble. A kind of distant low hum, and one which seemed to be coming closer.

George had to investigate – it was his duty as a vigilant and conscientious cat. He looked around to make sure there were no dogs in the vicinity – (it's always worth a check) – then jumped down into the lane. He started walking up the hill towards the noise, ears a-prick and primed to twitch and listen.

What *was* that noise? Was that low rumble – (no, it couldn't be!) – but was it the sound of *hooves*? Were there cows or horses here, in the two-legs' town?

George had only seen such animals once – and very large four-legs they were too – when, as a young kitten-cat, he had been taken by The Lady to visit friends in the countryside. So he didn't know much about such beasts really. But he knew for certain that their place was not here with cats and dogs and two-legs – they needed space and fields of grass to eat (*yeuch!*), not streets and houses and lanes.

George continued walking towards the sound. The rumble was coming – loud now – from over the brow of the hill. Just a few more paw-steps and he'd be there, and then he'd see what was making that noise.

He knew he couldn't turn back. It was his instinct to investigate, and his duty as a curious and conscientious cat. It was his natural need to know who or what was responsible for this commotion in the vicinity of his territory. For better or for worse.

When George reached the brow of the hill, he stopped dead, and his eyes almost popped out in shock.

For what he saw was a terrible thing – mice.

But not ordinary mice – not the tiny little long-tails that cats could easily catch in their quick claws and play with for hours, if they so desired, before eliminating them forever from the face of the earth.

Oh no, these were no ordinary mice. These were huge – the size of dogs, and big ones too. And as they came towards him, hundreds and hundreds of them, they let out the most dreadful, bloodcurdling sounds – growling and howling the wits out of poor old George. Because these mice sounded exactly like the worst sort of dogs – the ones who had a distinct taste and craving for cat flesh!

With his fur standing on end like a hedgehog's bristles, George turned and ran – down the lane, towards home. But no matter how hard he tried, he seemed to be getting nowhere, like running on ice, as if the lane had become some awful concrete conveyor belt.

The mouse-dog type monsters were soon upon him, licking his face with their long slobbering dog-tongues, tasting him for later, slurping sloppily over his face, about to bite into his beautiful fur coat – and preparing to *eat* him all up!

Then George woke up – for real, this time. It was dawn, and Dog was there, licking his face.

'By my paws!' said George, panting – he was horribly out of breath, 'What a terrible dream!'

George's dream was, for cats, just about as bad a dream as it was possible to have – except perhaps for the nightmare in which a cat turns into a dog (a common anxiety dream, as it happens).

'I... I... was just giving you a wash,' said Dog, 'There was... a snail... I think... on your fur... '

'Oh, right, splendid, well, thank you, little kitten-cat,' said George, 'We cats must look after each other at all times. It is good manners. It is *a rule*. Well done.'

Dog smiled proudly. He was pleased that what he was doing was right – because, if he was honest with himself, he didn't really know what he was doing at all. This, George might have told him in a candid moment, was a perfectly normal thing to feel. In fact, some two-legs never have a clue what they're doing either but never really seem to notice, no matter how often they are politely reminded.

George remembered now how he had allowed the kitten-cat to sleep next to him behind the shed that night, in a comfortable corner where they would remain completely dry and warm, even if it rained. Every cat needs such a secret place, just in case his usual home is suddenly out of bounds – which was the catastrophe that had, disgracefully, befallen George.

'Time... ' announced the old tom, 'for breakfast!'

And with that, he led the way towards the (now thankfully uncovered) cat flap and into the kitchen.

Dog followed him hesitantly, acutely aware that he was now doing that most personal of things – entering another cat's abode. This was something that should only be undertaken by explicit invitation, no matter how much uncouth and ill-brought-up cats may ignore such etiquette for reasons of personal greed and nourishment. In times of starvation and severe hunger, it is permissible to ignore such convention. But otherwise, as George had made clear as sky water, a personal invitation is an absolute must for a well-mannered and civilised cat.

Dog could see that there was a bowl in the kitchen piled with more food than he had ever seen in his whole little life. The bowl, he noticed, had the name 'GEORGE' written on its side in large bold letters.

The old tom miaowed his approval:

'The Lady, I am very pleased to say, always ensures that I am well-nourished and cared for – which is why, more often than not, I have plenty of rations to share. Double helpings. Triple, sometimes. A cat must always eat a good breakfast – one, at least, and possibly more on busy days. Please – tuck in.'

And, with that, the famished guest began gobbling up the food from one side of the bowl while George prepared to make a start on the other.

'Slowly, kitten-cat, slowly – take your time,' he said, 'We cats must never give the impression that we are desperately hungry, even if we are. It lets the species down.'

Dog swallowed, nodded, then resumed eating, this time at a casual and elegant pace, as befits a kitten-cat of noble and refined breeding.

He knew George was upset after recent events – knew too how he was worried and sad about The Man and what had happened to The Lady. But George was still kind enough to offer Dog his food at such a time – a selfless act of gracious and honourable feline generosity indeed.

Dog would never forget this, and made an extra-special effort to remember the memory, so he wouldn't forget either – something which momentarily made his face look a little bit strained and skewwhiff, just like when he was doing a mess.

Memory suitably stored, Dog stopped thinking and focused all his attentions on eating – which, for a kitten-cat, is highly recommended, and a good example of getting one's priorities absolutely right.

CHAPTER 8

Later that morning, George gave Dog a lesson on a necessarily essential activity in the daily routine of any successful feline:

'Now then, kitten-cat,' said George, 'Today's lesson is on the highly important cat activity of food consumption, otherwise known as eating.'

Dog sat up straight – even though, after scoffing such a huge breakfast, he really felt like lying down and having a jolly good nap.

'Now, pay attention very carefully, kitten-cat,' said George, and Dog pricked up his ears, 'As we all know, cats are capable of surviving in the wild – unlike two-legs, who would starve to skeletons out in the open within a few days. They just can't *mouse*, you see.'

'Too right, mate,' said Eric, who had just appeared on the wall.

'Good morning, Eric,' said Dog, with a happy little wag of his white-tipped tail.

'Ain't it just!' said Eric, with a wink, 'It's always a good mornin' when yer wake up soft 'n warm 'n fluffy and find out that you ain't snuffed it in the night!'

'Please, Eric,' said George, 'we have started a lesson

here. On eating, with which I know you need no assistance whatsoever.'

'Got it in one there, guv'nor… I mean… George.'

'Might I suggest that you practise the washing sequences we learnt yesterday?'

'You *might* suggest it, yeah… '

George gave Eric a very hard stare indeed.

'Oh alright alright, I'll do yer washing practice.'

'It is not *my* practice, Eric, it is yours. The kitten-cat here spent a good deal of time earlier this morning practising *his* washing.'

Dog nodded, because it was true. And the kitten could feel the evidence in his aching muscles. His back leg was still stiff after all that stretching, and his bottom a bit sore (though no cat would ever mention such a thing) from a thorough hygienic licking too.

'Alright alright, but I'm just doin' me face, not me wotzits – I'm still stiff as a cold dead cat after all that malarkey yesterday… '

Eric began licking his paw and smoothing it over his scruffy face with a wince. He winked his one eye at Dog – who, all in all, liked Eric very much, even though he knew he could be a bit cheeky and disrespectful at times.

'Right, let's press on,' said George, 'Eating… is a highly important thing for a cat. Together with sleeping and washing it makes up our Holy Trinity.'

Dog nodded three times – once for sleeping, once for washing, and once for eating – to help him remember them for later.

'Now, needless to say, there are some obvious points here. To wit, always eat delicately and with refinement. Never gobble. Wolfing down is not for cats, but for wolves and their descendants. We felines, unlike inferior four-legged species of the canine variety, are above that sort of thing.'

George cleared his throat. He could feel a tickly tuft of fur down there somewhere – but now was not the time or place for emetic activity, so he pressed on regardless despite the irritation, as all capable cats must.

'Eating too quickly can cause a cat to – and I use the vernacular here – *hick up*. This is something we all must resort to on occasion to expel accumulated fur from our gullets, an unfortunate and necessary consequence of thorough grooming whilst living in warm and comfy homes of course. But *hicking up* is an activity most certainly not to be encouraged or indeed caused by a cat himself through his own impatience and greed while eating, no matter how delicious the fare on offer.'

Dog blushed under his fur at the memory of his greedy eating at breakfast that morning. He'd try not to do it again, that was for sure.

'Now, of course, we cats – most of us, anyway – rely on our two-legs to provide for us. Two-legs, though, as I have already revealed, do not go mousing.'

Eric tutted as he washed his face with his paw, which made a snuffly sound a bit like a sneeze. Dog stifled a giggle. He was about to turn round to look at the stray, but thought better of it.

George, with something approaching super-cat level of patience, ignored Eric and carried on regardless.

'No, you see, two-legs have their own version of mousing. They go out and hunt down and/or gather a wide variety of food, which they then bring back home to share with us. This, I discovered after careful research, is what is known as *shopping*.'

'*Shop-ping*,' said Dog.

'Good. Right – moving on. We've got a lot to get through today.'

George puffed his chest out proudly – he was starting to enjoy this teaching lark. And, no matter how hopeless the task seemed, how dark and dismal the days ahead, he knew he had to believe that his course of action could work. That the kitten could, one day, grow up to be a quintessential cat, devoid of dreadful dogginess – the awful affliction that was making the kitten-cat's white-tipped tail wag happily in the air at that very moment, to the eternal shame of all cats.

'Remember,' miaowed George with suitable panache and poise, 'you are a cat. You deserve the best. Therefore, two-legs must be trained, for your ultimate benefit as well as theirs, to provide it for you. It might well be a fight to get the best, and it will never be easy. But if two-legs are eating well, then why shouldn't you?'

Eric gave a grunt of approval mid-wash. All that seemed perfectly reasonable to him, for those cats who had a thing for two-legs anyway, and who were thus prepared to put up with perpetual enslavement in return.

'Now, some two-legs may not need much training. They may already understand our needs, and their own duty to satisfy them, though often this is due to training by a dear departed feline from some unspecified time in the past.'

Sad wistful stares hung in the air for the briefest of moments. Cats always remembered and respected their ancestors and all departed fellow felines; even the scruffiest strays were careful to regularly acknowledge the enormous debt owed to their forebears.

George continued: 'Most, however, need to be

educated in how to behave appropriately so they know what is, and what is not, acceptable to us. And it never hurts to remind even the most experienced and benevolent two-legs of their obligations. Needless to say, there are some woefully misguided cats who will eat any old muck that their two-legs put in front of them – but kitten, this need not be you!'

Dog nodded hard. He was confident that he would not ever be one of those felines who settles for such shoddy treatment and poor quality rations – not if he studied hard about how to be an effective cat.

The kitten put up his paw – he had a question. George miaowed permission to speak.

'But how can we make them give us what we want, when it's the two-legs who decide what to give us to eat?'

Eric giggled at the kitten's ignorance – (his naivety was really so funny and sweet sometimes!) – then went quiet as another very hard stare was flashed in his direction.

'I'm glad you asked me that,' George went on, 'You see, if you are unfortunate enough to have a two-legs serve you disgusting muck instead of proper and decent quality food, then just go up to it and give it a good sniff – and possibly a poke with the nose. Even take a small mouthful – just one, mind. Then you give them *the look.*'

'*The… look*?' said Dog.

'Oh yes, *the look,*' said George, 'the look that says: *surely you cannot possibly expect me to eat THIS?* In complete silence too – no noise of any kind is necessary. No plaintive wails, no complaining cries and certainly no puppy-ish whimpers. Then walk away.'

'Walk… away?'

'Yes, walk away, no matter how hungry you are. The two-legs have to learn that serving such fare simply won't do – it won't do at all! Walk away and find a quiet corner somewhere – bed down, and say nothing. Not even if your stomach growls and groans.'

'And what happens next?' asked Dog, wide-eyed in wonder at this new knowledge.

'Why, nothing, of course. You just sit there, dozing if you like, for hours and hours. Soon – and this will happen, believe me – the two-legs will be able to bear it no longer. They will be worried. They will be upset. They will do anything to get you to eat something. And so will do what they should have done in the first place, and serve you some decent food – which, after all, they themselves are enjoying, so why shouldn't you?'

Dog felt his ignorance keenly, like a thorn in the paw. He had had so little real contact with two-legs – or other cats, for that matter – that he just didn't know any of this. But he was learning a lot today, thank goodness.

His tail flicked a secret wag in happiness at how well his lessons seemed to be going. And then he remembered that he really shouldn't have his tongue poking out like a puppy's, so popped it back into his mouth and closed his jaws tight to stop it flopping out again. George – who was observing it all – nodded approval at the kitten's self-correction.

'If they continue to serve you muck, refuse it. Remember – two-legs are a lot weaker than us. Therefore, your victory is assured in this battle of wills if you follow these instructions. And remember – you *must* win that first battle, because once it has been won you will have no further problems on the food front. But if you lose it – then, little kitten-cat, you will have condemned yourself to eating muck for the rest of your life – and I do not need to tell you how grave and grim a scenario *that* would be.'

George was right – it sounded absolutely horrid, and Dog wrinkled up his nose at the thought.

'Never accept anything less than total victory either, little kitten-cat. There can be no compromise when it comes to diet. It is simply not done.'

'Simply not done!' echoed Dog, nodding his determination for all to see. He was doing his best to remember everything, and was keen to put it into practice soon.

'Now, once you have trained your two-legs to consider your comfort and wellbeing at all times, they will be sure to offer you titbits and treats, especially if you remember to wake up and sit near them when they are in the process of preparing or consuming their own food. As a cat, of course, you will be able to smell this food scent from any area of your territory – something that they, with their primitive, inferior noses, will find simply amazing.'

Dog felt his nose glow with pride, and gave it a little twitch, as if to thank it for all its smelly help – and, well, just for *being there*.

'When you are offered a titbit or treat, it is important to remember your manners. Don't grab! Don't snatch! Don't gobble! Remember, you are not a wolf. You are not even a dog, thank goodness. Just accept the offering gently and tenderly, with love and gratitude, from the two-legs' blunt claws – the utterly useless appendages they call *fingers*.'

'*Fin-gers*,' mouthed Dog.

'Splendid!' miaowed George, and with that, he

closed his eyes and gave a great big yawn.

'I think, kitten-cat, that it is time for a mid-morning nap. All this talk of food has made me quite exhausted.'

Dog agreed, so curled up next to him by the shed. They each drifted off looking forward to lunch, for as George often said – *'it is never too soon to start thinking about your next meal'.*

Eric was already dozing, having given up on washing his face mid-whisker and closed his one bright eye to the world.

He had to admit, however, having listened to the lesson, that George was turning out to be an impressive teacher, and was pleasantly surprised that, even in a field in which he himself had quite some expertise – (food and the eating thereof) – even a self-sufficient and experienced stray like him was picking up a few tips.

CHAPTER 9

'George?' called a two-legs' voice, 'George? Where on earth have you got to?'

It was later that day, and The Lady had just arrived home.

'I think someone's calling you,' said Dog, who was sitting next to the old tom behind the shed.

George kept his eyes shut where he slouched, paws tucked under his substantial ginger-furred frame, ears not even slightly twitching at the sound.

There was no response, so Dog said it again:

'George, I think someone… '

'I know, kitten-cat, I know,' he groaned, 'The Lady.'

He sounded sleepy and lazy and almost too bored to make the effort to open his mouth, let alone say anything.

'But… ' asked Dog, 'shouldn't you… go and say hello… to your two-legs?'

This, George knew, was what decorum would demand – and this indeed is how he would usually behave, (and he was glad to see that his lessons were inculcating in the little kitten-cat the kind of respect for good manners to which each and every well-behaved and respectable cat should aspire).

But now, he knew, everything was different – because the day before The Lady had brought home that awful, rude, finger-in-the-stomach-poking two-legs – The Man – and there was no telling whether she had brought him back with her again.

'Do you want me to go and see if she's alone?' asked Dog.

George said nothing. A two-legs seeing him there behind the shed might have thought he was asleep, but Dog could tell that he was awake and could hear The Lady calling him loud and clear. His posture said it all. He was not going to be getting up or responding to The Lady because he just didn't want to – not unless Dog made him, that is.

'I think I'll go and have a look by myself then,' said Dog, the very image of a dog in a manger, even though he very definitely looked like a cat.

'No you will not!' said George, stretching his stiff paws and getting to his feet, 'You have no idea of the dangers which may be present. And besides, The Lady does not know you are here – and as she now seems to be under the control of that wicked Man two-legs, there's no telling what she might do.'

George walked towards the house. Dog followed.

'Stay here, kitten-cat, and that's an order.'

'But… '

'A well-mannered kitten-cat does not argue with his elders and betters,' cautioned George, a certain sternness stiffening his whiskers, 'I shall return presently to let you know if it is safe to come out. Then, later, we shall have dinner together. Is that clear?'

'Clear as sky water,' Dog nodded, and he watched George plod off towards the kitchen with slow and careful paw-prints, as is advisable for a cat of his mature years and well-padded plumpity.

'There you are, George!' said The Lady – she had, it seemed, returned home alone that afternoon.

'Miiiiiaaaaaooooow-owwwww-owwwww!' said George, *very* noisily indeed, so The Lady could not possibly be unaware of his feelings on the matter.

'Oh you noisy cat – come here now,' and with that, The Lady bent down and picked George up, hugging him close, and making him purr so thunderously that Dog could hear it loud and clear from behind the shed.

Later on, The Lady went out – (they heard the front door slam) – and Dog was invited inside to share dinner, as promised. He was pleased to see that George seemed much happier now, back in good spirits, not flat and deflated as he had been before.

'I am pleased to say,' announced George, pride sparkling in his eyes, 'that The Lady has seen sense at last and is back to her usual self, and without that awful Man two-legs.'

Dog listened as he enjoyed his dinner – a mouth-watering mix of succulent meats and sauces which was, he thought, just about the tastiest thing he had ever eaten.

'The Lady gave me a home when I was a kitten, specifically so that I would look after her, comfort her, guard her and love her,' said George, 'which I do to the very best of my ability as a dedicated and dutiful cat. Why on earth would she – *should she* – need anybody else?'

Dog chewed, swallowed and listened.

'The fact of the matter is that two-legs need us. Why, kitten-cat?'

'Errr... 'said Dog, his mouth full.

'Never mind never mind – finish your food. I shall tell you why.'

Dog nodded in gratitude and continued eating. Today's dinner really was delicious and he was very hungry indeed, what with all the excitement lately, and his being a growing kitten-cat too.

'The fact of the matter is, little kitten-cat, all two-legs are lonely. Not always, of course, but on a pretty regular basis. And not just those two-legs who live alone either. Strange as it may seem, the two-legs who live together in the same place as others are often the loneliest of them all.'

This was very confusing to Dog, so he asked a very big question, using a very small word he had learnt when he was an even smaller kitten:

'But *why?*' he said, instinctively aware that this was a very big question indeed, though he wasn't sure exactly how – or *why*, for that matter...

'We,' said George, 'are cats. That means that we are – amongst other things – beautiful, honourable, dignified, elegant, self-contained, intelligent, charming and sweet. We are the paragon of animals – the noblest of known species. This is a well-accepted fact, not just an old tom's opinion.'

Dog chewed his food with pride. It was so great to know he was a member to the best species there was, even if he was a little puppyish with it. Just think, he could have been born *anything* at all – even a two-legs, if he'd been really unlucky.

'I say this not to boast,' continued George, 'but merely to state the obvious. Two-legs are not like us. They lack our self-sufficiency – our solitary survival skills – and so they constantly struggle to bear their loneliness. That is why – or is at least one big reason why – they need us.'

George was full, having eaten very well earlier that day, but the food on the plate did look well up to the requisite standards and really rather delicious. The Lady had, as usual, put out so much that it seemed rude not to make the effort to find room for a teeny bit more.

No cat ever knows – not for certain, anyway – where his next meal is coming from, when the summer glut will freeze into the famine of winter. So whenever the opportunity for feeding presents itself, every cat has a survival duty to grasp it with all paws – irrespective of how shoddily he is being treated by his two-legs at the time.

Or, as George was wont to say at moments such as these: *'There's no use cutting off your tail to spite your bottom.'*

'So,' said Dog, concentrating hard, 'is it… *good* that two-legs are so lonely?'

'Kitten-cat,' miaowed George, finishing off a mouthful, 'it is not our place to judge whether this state of affairs is good or bad. We are merely innocent participants in the process. We cats do what we can, in the circumstances. It's hardly our fault that we have evolved to be the superior species, is it?'

The kitten never really thought of himself as being part of the superior species before meeting George, but the way he put it – stating that cats did in fact occupy that lofty evolutionary position – all just seemed to make the most perfect sense somehow. He was certainly learning a great many wonderful things today!

'I don't suppose it is,' said Dog.

'No, it *definitely* isn't our fault. It is *never* our fault, because as cats, we are always blameless.'

'*Blame-less*,' repeated Dog, practising the new word so he'd be sure to remember it. George nodded his approval.

'But never forget, kitten-cat, that the basic and constant loneliness of two-legs is the prime reason why every cat has the home and service he wants in the first place. Without it, we are doomed.'

'*Doomed*,' mouthed Dog. It was another new word – and one that sounded very scary, like the yawning call of a wolf echoing through the trees of some dark and dangerous forest.

He hoped he'd remember them all and not get mixed up, because he wasn't used to learning new words very much. In fact, until meeting George, he couldn't remember learning any, though he supposed he must have done, somehow, or he wouldn't have been able to miaow at all. But how, and when, this learning occurred was a complete mystery.

'Splendid!' said George, 'You see, their weakness is the basis of our strength. It is the way things are, the way things were, and the way things ever shall be too.'

George thought he'd end it there, and focused his attention instead on the bowl of fresh water next to his food. He began lapping it up with delicate licks – teaching was turning out to be very thirsty work indeed!

Suddenly, the sound of a key turning in the front door made both Dog and George freeze mid-mouthful.

She was back!

Then the voices – that of The Lady, but also the deep booming baritone of The Man.

He was back too!

'Quick!' said George, struggling to swallow his food, 'Behind the shed, kitten-cat!'

'But what about you?' asked Dog.

'Never mind about me. There comes a time in every cat's life when he has to make a stand. And that time is come.'

The two-legs' voices were growing louder as they approached the kitchen.

'Leave, kitten-cat! Now!'

As instructed, Dog hurtled through the cat flap at speed – using the most solid part of his head as a battering ram so as not to cause any lasting damage.

Within seconds he was sitting behind the shed, out of breath, and with a sort of dizzy, fuzzy feeling between his ears, wondering what would happen to George now he was alone in the house with The Lady and The Man, awaiting his fate.

CHAPTER 10

'Miiiiiaaaaaoooooowwwwww!!!!' said George, in no uncertain terms, as The Lady entered the kitchen.

'Miiiiiaaaaaoooooowwwww-owwwwww-owwwwww!!!'

And then, when The Man followed her into the room, the ginger tom let out an almighty hiss at him:

'Hsssssssssssssssssssssssssss!!!'

George looked up at The Lady, pleading for her to see the danger she was in.

'Miiiiiaaaaaoooooowwwww-purrrrup-purrrrup,' he reiterated, the little chirrup at the end a memory of happier days, when The Lady would arrive home alone, unaccompanied by this new unwelcome invader.

George hoped The Lady could understand what he was saying. She was usually good at that – for a two-legs anyway. She was even fairly good at working out what he wanted to say even if he didn't say anything – the hang of a tail and the demeanour of whiskers and face seemed to suffice. But on this occasion George made it absolutely clear what he wanted to say in a very loud and uncompromising manner:

'Miiiiiaaaaaoooooowwwww-owwwwww-owwwwww!!!' he said, again.

'George, please! What on earth's got into you, you noisy cat?'

'Maybe the old mog's just going a bit senile. Y'know, doolally. Loopy-loo. Happens to us all, old age… Be kinder to put 'em out of their misery really.'

'Cats or people?' wondered The Lady aloud.

The Man said nothing. Instead, he lit a cigarette and proceeded to puff the smoke in and out in a manner which made him resemble an old cold cat breathing the frost of winter.

'I don't know, he doesn't *seem* ill,' said The Lady, reaching down to feel the coldness of George's nose, 'And he's eating well – more than usual, I think, though it's hard to tell. I've always said he must have hollow legs!'

'Prob'ly pregnant!' sniggered The Man, 'Happened to a rabbit at our school when I was a kid. We all thought it was a boy bunny. But then it started getting fatter and fatter. And when it gave birth even the headmistress had to admit that it was a girl! Ever had old George here properly sexed by a vet?'

'Oh *he's* not a *she*,' said The Lady, 'Definitely… I mean… definitely not. We had him, you know, *done*… years ago.'

'Maybe he's sort of in-between – half girl, half boy. It happens. The hormones can play havoc once they've lost their fundamentals. He could be a trans-cat!'

At this point, George had had more than enough of being insulted and abused in his own home:

'I most certainly do *not* have hollow legs, and am *not* eating for two either, though I may invite guests to share my fare from time to time. And as for being a she-cat or a *trans-cat* or pregnant or… anything else… how *very dare* you!!!'

This came out as: 'Miiiiiaaaaaooooowww-wowwww-wowwww-yow-yow-waaaaahhhhh-waaaaahhhhhwwwww-miaow-miaow-miiiiioooooaaaa awwwww!!!'

The Lady didn't understand a word. But Dog did. He could hear every miaow and yowl from where he sat, all ears, skulking behind the shed outside.

'Cor, what a racket!' said The Man, 'No wonder I'm more of a dog person – it's quieter!'

'Pick me up!' yelled George at The Lady, 'Please please please, pick me up! Then I can tell you *everything!*'

But his plaintive cries went unheeded. Instead, The Lady made her way out of the kitchen.

'Just going up to have a shower and get changed. What time's the restaurant booked?' she called, on her way upstairs.

'Don't worry – we've got all the time in the world,' The Man shouted after her. He then turned to George:

'Haven't we, Georgy-porgy?'

There was a nasty snide grin smeared across his face.

The old tom turned and headed towards the cat flap – but it was too late. The Man had him by the tail.

He pulled George towards him, reeling him in like a fish, tugging his tail until he could make a grab for the belly. By now, George was – he was sorry to say – trapped.

The Man then picked him up, being careful to keep hold of the tom's front paws so that he couldn't – no matter how hard he tried – get his claws free to scram and scratch and defend himself.

And so it was that George found himself in the position that all cats dread: helpless and at the mercy of others. He had lost control.

'Now look, fatso,' said The Man, holding George up to his face, a smouldering 'smoke-stick' still protruding from his mouth, 'If you scram me again, it's straight down the knackers' yard for you, moggy. D'you hear me? Should be able to make quite a few tennis rackets what with all the spare cat gut you've got here – eh, fatty-boom-boom?!!!'

The Man sneered a fearless laugh. His bony fingers dug into the tom-cat's ample tummy like claws.

George said nothing. His heart was beating fast as nightmares in his chest. He was now face to face with The Man, a creature whose breath stank black as smoke, as if his innards were burning – as if he were the very devil himself.

'Just once more, ginger, and you're *out*!' said The Man, 'Got it, mog?'

George growled low – a deep guttural growl reserved especially for moments of great crisis and unpleasantness.

Then The Man poked George again in the stomach – hard – jabbing him in a most cruel and heartless, (not to mention painful), manner.

'Fat fat fat fat *fat*!' chanted The Man, with a stab of his finger into George's guts for every word, 'Time we put you on a diet to fight the flab, eh?'

And with that, The Man leant down to the bowl of food, and somehow managed to pick it up and place it on the kitchen work surface, all while holding an immobilised George flat against his body.

'That,' he said, nodding at the bowl of food, 'is going straight in the bin – and you, Georgy-porgy pudding and pie, are so out of here, fleabag!'

The Man then opened the back door, took a step

forward and threw – actually *threw* – George out into the garden.

The tom sailed through the air, twisting and turning as he prepared for the inevitable hard landing.

And then he landed – hard – on the garden path, his old arthritic legs straining with the pain of his not inconsiderable weight.

The Man laughed. George regained his composure and gave his fur a reassuring lick before hobbling off to behind the shed with what was a new and noticeable limp. The dog-end of a cigarette followed George's trajectory into the garden, where it lay smouldering at the edge of the path, like hate.

Eric was observing all this from behind the hedge in the neighbours' garden, from where Dog was also keeping his head down, watching developments – the kitten had moved there from behind the shed when he heard the back door open. They both now knew that, whatever jealousy George had felt towards The Man, his animosity was indeed justified. This two-legs had proven himself to be a very bad two-legs indeed.

'Shhhhh!' whispered Eric, making sure Dog didn't give himself away.

The Lady only thought she had one cat, George – (as did The Man) – and didn't realise her garden was also now home to a kitten-cat called Dog, and occasionally also to a stray called Eric and a well-travelled *sophisti-cat* called François. And that wasn't even counting visiting neighbours, like Fifi, and some of the others who walked along the wall on their patrols.

It was therefore their duty to stay as quiet as mice – even though they were cats. Which all sort of made sense, somehow, maybe, though perhaps it shouldn't have – when Eric thought about it. This was exactly why he tried not to think too much – it always gave him the most dreadful of headaches and, what was perhaps even worse, tended to leave him considerably more confused than he had been to start with.

When they were absolutely sure that The Man was out of the kitchen, Eric led Dog through the hedge, along the wall, and down into The Lady's garden. A quick spray by Eric extinguished the smouldering 'smoke stick' with an efficient hiss. Then they went up along the side of the shed, where George was sitting tenderly licking his leg in sad and solitary silence.

'Are… are you alright, George?' asked Dog.

He had seen how badly the old tom had been limping when he'd walked towards the shed. But only a cat himself knows how badly – or not – he is hurt. It is impossible for observing cats to really know the extent of a fellow feline's injuries.

Needless to say, two-legs are, almost without exception, utterly clueless in such matters, thinking (as they tend to) that the most minor of injuries is serious, and that the most painful and sore of ailments is nothing at all to worry about.

As Eric always said, 'If they's as bad at knowin' their own health as what they are wiv ours, then s'no wonder they all looks as miserable as *dead-ified* dogs all day long… '

'No serious damage done,' announced George, his tongue flattening his fur back into place. Dog could see now that it was wet and thinned with licking – he could glimpse a nasty graze on one of his back legs, and several developing bruises too.

'Cat your age's gotta be careful,' said Eric, unwisely.

George stopped grooming himself and gave the stray a long hard stare.

'I landed on all four feet,' said George, 'Therefore, I have suffered merely minor abrasions. Look and learn, kitten-cat. Landing on all four paws is an absolute necessity for survival for all cats in any circumstances. Forget that, and you could suffer serious injury – a sprain, a breakage, or worse. Remember it, and you *will* survive.'

'You's not wrong there, George,' Eric butted in, 'I remember once when I's on the window-sill of an 'ouse, and some two-legs or uvver opened the window! Down down down I went – prob'ly 'undreds and 'undreds of cat miles… '

George closed his eyes. He had a real headache by now and did not want to listen to Eric's shaggy dog stories. As it happened, he never wanted to listen to such tom-fluffery even under normal circumstances – and probably wouldn't have wanted to if they were shaggy cat stories either. But now most definitely was not the best time.

'Eric,' snapped George, 'Don't exaggerate!'

'Straight up!' said Eric, 'And I landed on all four paws and so I'm still 'ere! Just weren't my time to snuff it, eh? Another life *gawn*… '

'I'm going on my rounds,' miaowed George, 'Kitten-cat, you stay here. Eric, you look after him while I'm gone. The Man is still in the house and could do *anything*.'

'Righty-ho,' said Eric, knowing when to take an order from a superior cat, especially one who had been treated so terribly by a two-legs. 'I'll keep an eye out for 'im? An eye out, eh? *Geddit?*'

Eric theatrically winked his solitary seeing eye at the old tom, but he was clearly in no mood for jokes.

They watched George limp off to the end of the garden, jump up onto the wall (which was a bit of a struggle), and walk along it towards the neighbours' garden to start his tour of the outlying territories.

'A cat's gotta do his patrol,' said Eric, 'Even when he's not feelin' up to it in his whiskers, like.'

Dog nodded, slowly and seriously. It made him unhappy to see George in so much pain.

How he wished that he hadn't eaten so much of George's food! After hearing The Man call George 'fat', and all sorts of other horrid things, because of how much food had gone from his bowl, pangs of guilt nibbled at the kitten's tummy like itchy, invisible mice.

'I hope he's going to be alright,' miaowed Dog, ears drooping in dismay.

'Old George? Course he will!' said Eric, 'Just give him time. It ain't his legs what's hurting most neither… '

Dog looked puzzled – he had seen for himself the painful graze on George's leg.

'Pride, little kitten-cat, pride… '

'Oh, like lions?' said Dog.

He had heard all about prides of lions from George in a lesson – the one about extended family, the importance of knowing one's roots and the consequent superiority bestowed on all members of the species.

'Yeah,' agreed Eric, 'Like lions, if you wants… Hurt pride can be more painful than just about anyfink else. And so can jealousy.'

'You mean, George is… '

'Jealous? Course he is! He loves The Lady, and The Lady loves 'im, and now that there's an uvver two-legs in the 'ouse, there ain't no room for no-one else. I means that The Lady can only love one of 'em at a time – and at the moment, it ain't George.'

Dog felt sad as sky water. He knew how much George loved The Lady, and how cruelly he had been thrown out of the house by The Man. It just didn't seem fair.

'See, that's why I steers well clear of two-legs. They always lets you down in the end, in some way or uvver. Always hurts you, they does – if you lets 'em love you, and you makes the mistake of lovin' 'em back.'

Dog wasn't sure he agreed with this; but on the other paw, he really didn't know what to think. It was all most confusing. And he knew just how baffling it was by how far his tongue was sticking out.

Learning how to be a cat was turning out to be much more difficult than he could possibly have imagined.

Eric sighed:

'Two-legs ain't got no idea how unhappy they make us cats. No idea at all. They's a very *hignorant* species, if you asks me, at the end of the day… '

And with that, even though it wasn't the end of the day quite yet, Eric closed his one good eye and curled up for a nap.

'I'm *exhaust-ificated!*' he yawned, *'Knacker-ified!* Totally *tired-ified,* in uvver miaows. This feline needs a bit o' *rest-bite* and *recuprification,* if you knows what I mean, kitten.'

'Oh I do, Eric,' yawned Dog, imitating the stray, 'I'm… *exhaust-ified* and… *knacker-ficated* as well!'

Eric chuckled, sneezed and then yawned over his paws:

'Old George is learnin' you a lot, kitten-cat, so you

makes sure you listens to 'im and gets yourself *heducated*. You could grow up to be one of the sharpest claws in the paw, kitten – if you listens, like, an' works yer whiskers off… '

'Oh I will, Eric, I will… ' replied the kitten-cat – but the stray was already snoring, fast asleep.

Dog closed his eyes, wishing things could be back to the way they were. He hoped his hardest that George would be able to get back to his old self again and teach him more about how to be a proper cat. And he was doing his best to be one – he really was.

But the truth of the matter was that the more Dog learnt about being a cat, the less he realised he knew. It was very confusing indeed – and not a little worrying.

Dog went to sleep with his little pink tongue poking out like a puppy's, though his usually waggly tail was as still as his whiskers with the sadness of it all.

CHAPTER 11

'Right, kitten-cat, time for another lesson,' said George.

He was back from his trot and looking, if not exactly relaxed, then marginally less ruffled and tense than he had before going on his rounds. He was still rather befuddled and grumpy, though – sort of *'befuddergrumped'* – but that was perfectly understandable, considering.

'Bit late in the day to start more *heducation*, innit?' said Eric.

'I have warned you before, stray. I am the teacher. The kitten-cat is the student. You are here only because of our generosity of spirit. You are therefore beholden to behave with good grace and manners, and to defer to the discipline of the class, should you wish to remain.'

Eric wasn't sure he understood all the words George was using – some of them were awfully big and didn't even sound like proper Cat words. But they sounded as though they were in more or less the right order, so it seemed fair enough to him.

'Right you are, guv'nor… I mean… George,' he said, and then added, 'Sorry,' which was perhaps the only reason he was allowed to stay for the lesson.

'Now then,' harrumphed George, ensuring the attention of the class, 'Our lesson this evening concerns the process of suspending consciousness – or 'sleeping', as it is generally known. Needless to say, sleeping is a highly important aspect of any cat's day. Together with eating and washing, it is one of the three corners of the perfect triangle of our lives – our Holy Trinity. No time spent pursuing it is thus ever time truly wasted.'

'It's the gleesome threesome, innit?' said Eric with a wink. George ignored him, but Dog couldn't help himself giving a little giggle.

'Sleep,' said George.

Dog wondered if it was an order – he was ready to close his eyes, if instructed, at any time.

'What is it for? Where does it come from? Why do we need it? Three questions that no cat will ever need to answer, so three questions that can be entirely discounted at the outset.'

Eric grinned. This was turning into his kind of lesson – one in which it was completely unnecessary to learn anything, do anything or think anything at all. If only all education were more like this – (though apparently a fair amount was, so he'd heard) – then he might have made more effort when he was a kitten.

'All you have to remember,' continued George, 'is that, no matter how you sleep – in which position, for example, whether on your side, stretched out, or curled into a fluffy bundle, squared neatly with paws tucked under, or even on your back with paws hanging limp – and this one is particularly effective when lying on a lap – the two-legs like us when we're sleeping. They just can't help it: they love us unconscious! And fortuitously, we just can't help having this effect either – we are, after all, so exceedingly sweet and adorable when in repose. The sight of us sleeping, or even just cat-napping, makes two-legs feel good – about us, about themselves, about everything. Pay attention now, kitten-cat.'

'Sorry,' said Dog – his eyes were starting to close. He was feeling a bit *exhaust-ificated*, if truth be told, and all this talk of sleep really wasn't helping.

'It's been a long day, I know, but we need to finish this now to keep the curriculum on track.'

Neither Dog nor Eric knew what a 'curriculum' was, but they were keen to keep it on track anyway, as that seemed the best place for it by far.

'Particularly effective is the pose, thus – observe!' and George lay down on the ground pretending to sleep with his paws over his eyes, 'Or… thus,' and he moved his paws to be over his nose, 'Resting one's head on one's body – or one's legs, for example, front or back – is also recommended.'

Dog watched this pose closely and mimicked it in mirror-image.

'Splendid, kitten-cat,' said George, 'You're proving to be a quick learner, I must say.'

'An old tom once told me,' said Eric, 'that them two-legs, they sometimes finds it hard to sleep. Is that right, guv'nor?'

George gave a wry chuckle. It all sounded very strange to Dog who, in common with all cats, had never had any trouble falling asleep and struggled somewhat to grasp the whole concept of sleeplessness.

'Is it true?' he asked, with a disbelieving shudder. It sounded very odd, like some strange myth made up to frighten kittens.

'Yes, I'm afraid it is,' George sighed, 'It's called "insomnia".'

'*In-som-ni-a*,' mouthed Dog. He was keen to learn more big words.

'*In... son... mi... ahhh*,' echoed Eric, concentrating hard.

'Insomnia is a debilitating condition from which, it should be remembered proudly, no cat has ever been known to suffer,' continued George, 'But the most marvellous thing is that we cats are so good at relaxing two-legs that we can assist them in overcoming this dreadful affliction.'

Dog thought this strange sleepless state-of-affairs all sounded too peculiar to be true, but was prepared to take George's word for it.

The lesson continued:

'Never – ever – allow yourself to become sleep-deprived, kitten-cat, for that way disaster lies. Your concentration will go, as will your strength and agility, and all tasks attempted will suffer as a result. We cats must have our sleep. I, for example, am utterly useless if I don't get my sixteen hours a day.'

'More like seventeen for me, guv'nor,' miaowed Eric, yawning a yawn so wide that no cat present properly understood what he was saying anyway.

'Precise needs vary from cat to cat, but anything less than you need will cause sleep deprivation and catastrophe – if you'll pardon the pun – so be careful, kitten. Being a cat is a very tiring business indeed.'

'Them two-legs is weird, I'll give 'em that,' said Eric, wondering what on earth a 'pun' was and whether he could eat it. He stretched out to his full length and rolled in the nasturtiums, squashing three worms in the process, which were now stuck with slime to his long shaggy fur in a manner that made them resemble nothing so much as decorations on a rather unusual Christmas tree.

Dog wasn't sure how much sleep he needed. He never kept track really – he just slept, woke up, then slept again, then woke up again, then slept again, and so on. Consequently, he had never really given it much thought. But now he was giving it lots, and that could mean only one thing – he was getting a good education.

Dog was so grateful that George, despite his hurt pride and suffering, kept soldiering on in this way, making sure nothing was left out of his studies. And the kitten was doing his best, he really was, though it was just so difficult to give up all the wagging and the yapping and the tongue-poking!

One day, he'd be able to repay the debt. One day…

'They are the inferior species, it's true,' said George, 'though it would not be the done thing for a polite cat to dwell on the point… '

Eric, however, was not a polite cat.

'S'like, when they wants to wash, they don't do what we does – oh no! They takes off all their false fur, which they has to wear coz of some well nasty *horrible-ifying* skin problem what makes 'em bald all over, and then they sits for ages in a big long bowl full of their own dirty water!'

'Yeeeuuukkkk!' said Dog, who thought it all sounded quite disgusting.

'Straight up,' said Eric, 'and if you ever sees 'em doing it, you'll see that they ain't got much fur at all, and what fur they does 'ave, is in all the wrong places – the places what is all hot and sweaty – which is *hexactly* the places where we cats ain't got 'ardly no fur at all!'

Dog was amazed – his tongue poked out in confusion at all these strange stories. They sounded almost incredible, as if some storytelling cat had made them all up.

'Is it true?' he asked.

George was reluctant to say anything. He didn't much like criticising two-legs too severely, not after how good The Lady had been to him – especially as he loved her more than anything else in the world. It was not their fault that they had strange and peculiar instincts and habits; and two-legs' idiosyncrasies (of which there were oh-so-many) surely merited sympathy more than mockery or condemnation?

'There are many things about two-legs that we may find strange,' said George, 'but... '

'Strange?' interrupted Eric, 'Stark raving dog-bonkers, more like! They's got smell-rooms where they does their spray which is also where they does their washin' – *in hexactly the same place!* How disgusting is that?'

'Yeeeuuukkk!' shuddered Dog.

'Don't they even know that you gotta spray as far away as possible from where you does your washin'? It's madness, I tells yer. Madness!'

'It is the two-legs' way, Eric,' explained George, 'We cats must be tolerant and accommodating.'

'And sometimes, them two-legs goes to all the trouble o' diggin' the soil in their gardens, making a really lovely natural litter tray, and then – *and then* – they just leaves it and goes instead and does their spray and mess in their smell-rooms!'

'Yeeeuuukkk!' miaowed Dog, appalled.

'*Hexactly*! But that don't stop 'em getting all upset

when we uses them outside litter trays what they've made in their gardens. Oh no, take it from me, kitten, they's all dog-bonkers mad, them two-legs, and you's better off without 'em.'

'Stuff and nonsense!' snapped George, 'Eric, you really must try to control your outbursts and be more understanding. I am trying to teach the kitten how to be a proper cat and how to do what most normal, healthy felines do, which is find a two-legs to look after. I'd therefore appreciate it if you didn't keep trying to undermine the process with your cynical stray cat contributions.'

'My opinion is my opinion, George.'

'Indeed, but if you *could* keep it to yourself, for the sake of the kitten-cat, then that would be exceedingly helpful.'

Just then, François appeared on the wall and jumped down into the garden.

'Sacrebleu!' he gasped, sounding out of breath, 'Zut alors! I 'ave for you zer news most terrible, mes amis!'

'What is it, François?' said George, 'Whatever's the matter?'

'It eez zer Lady… '

George's ears pricked up like whiskers at the words.

'She eez in zer danger most big. We must to 'elp her, Georges. C'est *un grand catastrophe!*'

George and Eric and Dog gathered around François, sitting down in a semi-circle, ears a-prick, as he began telling his tale.

CHAPTER 12

'It has *'appen-ed* when I was sit on zer roof, nearby to zer window of zer sleep-room of zer Lady. I have seen somesink most sérieux. Zut alors!'

George, Eric and Dog listened intently. François was not one to exaggerate events and so whatever he had seen must have been serious indeed.

'But before ziss, I must to confess to somesink, Georges,' he said.

'Oh?' said George, who wasn't sure he liked the sound of this, 'Go on.'

'I must to apologise, mon ami. I sought you 'ave been jealous of ziss new Man two-legs, zat what you say about him was zer jealousy who was speaking seulement. I sought you were, peut-être... 'ow you say?... *imaginating* all zeez bad sings about 'im... '

'I most certainly was not, François. I just knew that The Man two-legs was a wrong 'un as soon as he stepped into my domain!'

'Oui, je le sais... and I am know zat zer Lady she means to you a great deal, and zat eez why I am apologise to you. It was not a *figgy-ment* of zer imagination of Georges, bien sur.'

'I can assure you, as a fellow cat of dignity and honour, that it was not!'

'Non, now I know ziss,' François went on, 'But 'ow do we know zat what we see eez zer realité, or if it eez just zer dream – a *figgy-ment* of zer imagination, an illusion of our existence which eez, peut-être, not so real. En effet, 'ow do we know zat we exist at all, non? Maybe everysing we see eez only zer dream, in zer mind of zer cat who is a-sleeping in some place far far away? C'est possible, non?'

And with that, François gazed at the sky, looking most philosophical and existentialist, in a feline sort of way.

Eric, meanwhile had already closed his one good eye and put his paws over his ears – what this exotic tabby was saying was making his head spin and giving him a splitting headache.

George said nothing: he knew what these foreign cats could be like, so let François carry on.

Dog was about to yap a question at George, before remembering that cats don't yap, so instead chose to say nothing – partly because he couldn't even remember what the 'something' was any more...

'So I sought maybe zat Georges he was just jealous, zat zer bad sings zat he was see in ziss Man two-legs was just zer 'allucination, zer fantasy who eez caused by the jealousy of Georges, because he eez love zer Lady so much.'

'I can assure you once again,' said George, 'that it most certainly was not any hallucination on my part.'

'Too right,' agreed Eric, 'The Man chucked him out the house an' all – *pained* his paws, *limpified* his leg!'

'Just a scratch, Eric. I'll live... '

'I sought zat Georges was being a bit... ow you say?... *under zer bottom.*'

'Over the top,' sighed George, weary at all the bad Cat grammar and syntax his ears had had to suffer lately.

'Ah oui, over zer top – and *under zer bottom.*'

'But The Man – he *is* bad, isn't he?' asked Dog.

'Ah oui, mon petit, zer Man, he eez most bad, certainement.'

'So... ' said George, 'You were on the roof, and... '

'Oui, Georges,' continued François, 'I was on zer roof, and zen I climb down to the sill of zer window of zer sleep-room of zer Lady... '

There were a lots of 'ofs' in that sentence. Eric and Dog had just about worked out what it meant when François carried on with the story:

'Zer Lady, she went to do zer washing... in zer room of smell – comme d'habitude, malheureusement – and zer Man two-legs he eez stay down zer stairs.'

'Yes,' said George, getting impatient, 'and?'

'Mais non, mon ami – zer Man he does not stay down zer stairs. He go up zer stairs, and I see him go into zer sleep room of zer Lady when she eez in zer room of smell.'

'I knew it!' said George, 'I mean, what kind of two-legs would enter another's sleep-room uninvited?'

'Mais non, zat eez not all.'

The cats huddled close around François, whisker to whisker, as his miaow voice diminished into a soft hush of a whisper.

'Zer Man, he has *creep*... '

'*Crept*, François, *crept*... '

'C'est ça – he has *crept* into zer sleep-room of zer

Lady, an' he has open zer drawer in zer way most quiet, and he has take out zer sings who eez shiny… '

'Shiny things?' asked George.

'Oui – shiny sings,' said François.

Dog remembered watching some fish swimming around in a stream once, and they looked very shiny – so were they the shiny things? But why would The Lady keep fish in her sleep-room?

George turned to Dog.

'You see, kitten-cat. It may sound strange but two-legs, especially the females, wear these *shiny things* called 'jewellery'– on their paws, round their necks… '

'Oh yeah!' said Eric, 'You means them jingling cat toys what they dangle from their ears. I remember once this she-two-legs got well hissy when I cuffed 'em one! But why wear 'em if you don't want us to play wiv 'em? Mad, y'see, kitten-cat – they's all barkin' dog-bonkers, all them two-legs… '

'Shhh, Eric,' said George, raising a paw to Dog so he wouldn't interrupt with any more questions, 'Go on, François.'

'So, zer Man he 'as take many of zer shiny sings and he 'as putted zem dans la poche… 'ow you say?… in zer pocket.'

'A thief!' said George, 'I knew it!'

'Zer Lady was in zer smell-room and zen she eez come out, and zer Man eez again down zer stairs and zen zey go out. But zer Lady does not know zat zer Man 'as take zer shiny sings. '

'A veritable thief!' yelled George, unable to keep his miaows down any more.

'And zen, I am hear zer Man talking on zer sing two-legs carry in zer poches – he has hold ziss sing to his ear and he has talk about zer "rich pickings". And zen he has *rubb-ed* zee 'ands, like ziss.'

François rubbed his two front paws together in an image of the utmost greed and covetousness, as though washing them with soap and water in the most disgusting two-legs manner.

'An' zer Man, he has laugh, comme ça... '

And François gave the most *wickedest*, the most *devilish*, the most *evilest* laugh that his vigorous miaowing could produce:

'Haa-haaarghhhh-heehaahaa-haaarrgghh-heeheehaahaarghrghrghhhhh!'

Usually, George didn't approve of cats imitating two-legs. It always ended in mockery and abuse, hissing and spitting, and goodness knows what else. It was just so *common*, and well below the dignity expected of any decent well-bred feline. However, there were always times for exceptions to the rule...

'I knew it! I knew he was a wrong 'un from the first time I saw him,' miaowed George, suddenly animated and puffed up with the rightness of his intuition, 'It's the smell, you know – I can always sniff a wrong 'un. Oh yes... '

This was true. It was an indisputable fact, well-known even by the dimmest of two-legs, that cats have a sense of smell way superior to that of the inferior species they look after.

'We cats can smell things that two-legs cannot smell at all, thanks to our exceedingly well-developed olfactory sense,' said George, 'yet another reason that we, as the superior species, have a duty to look after those less fortunate than ourselves.'

'Two-legs, you mean?' Dog asked.

'The very same! They are inferior in so many ways, so we must do our duty and help them to overcome their evolutionary failings. It is not their fault, after all.'

'Thass a matter of opinion,' muttered Eric, doing a smell.

Dog knew that The Lady was lucky to have a cat like George and just couldn't understand why she would want to do something so awful as spend so much time with another two-legs – it seemed so ungrateful, somehow.

George continued:

'We can also hear things that two-legs have never heard, and cannot ever hear because of their inherited hearing problem. Our ears can hear the distant cries of cats and other animals, the slightest rustle of leaves in the wind, and even the tiniest tread of a mouse's paws from a very great distance. Two-legs, on the other hand, can't even hear us coming.'

'Ah oui,' said François, 'c'est vrai, ça.'

'Too right, an' all!' said Eric with a wink.

'And two-legs' sense of smell is woefully inferior too, though they can sniff at a primitive and basic level. So look after your nose and your ears, kitten-cat, and they will always be your best friends.'

Dog licked his paw and gave his ears – and then his nose – a little wash. How fortunate he was to have been born feline, and not a member of an inferior two-legged species! He simply couldn't imagine life without the superior qualities of a cat.

Earlier that day, Dog had heard The Lady tell The Man that she thought George smelt of toast, (something George himself thought was just about as ridiculous as most thoughts two-legs have), and Dog wondered if he smelt the same.

His teacher told him that: 'no, he didn't smell of toast'. But then neither did George, according to George – it was just two-legs' terrible sense of smell getting all mixed up again.

But he did tell Dog that all cats had their own individual smell – a smell they should be proud of, a smell that was one of the best communication tools they possessed.

Two-legs also had their individual smells, of course, but had no idea how to use them, making them utterly useless – to two-legs anyway. But cats used these smells all the time to identify two-legs – (well they did all look more or less the same!) – and assess their health and wellbeing.

Eric, so George said, smelt in a way that no respectable cat ever should. Dog had noticed this too – because the stray smelt of the slimy puddles that form at the bottom of dustbins, which is not a nice smell at all.

François, being a well-travelled cat, naturally carried with him the exotic perfume of herbs and spices from distant lands, in a most pleasant – if a little musky – way.

And Dog?

Well, according to his teacher, the kitten smelt of 'hope and expectation', which didn't seem to make sense until George told him he also smelt of 'newly-fallen sky water', which sort of made more sense really – to Dog, anyway.

George was just about to tell François, and the other cats there, that he had a plan – (though the details still needed to be slept on somewhat) – when Fifi appeared on the wall.

CHAPTER 13

'Mademoiselle Fifi... ' purred François, 'Beautiful *beautiful* Mademoiselle Fifi. Your fur eez so soft and smooth like zer silk, your eyes zey shine like zer stars most bright een zer sky... '

'Alright alright, that's quite enough of that sort of thing,' grumped George, 'May I remind you whose garden and wall this is?'

'Your coat she eez so beautiful and black like zer night who eez dark... '

'Miss Fifi,' miaowed George, 'please accept my... our... heartfelt apologies for the deplorable display of doggery that you were unfortunate enough to witness yesterday.'

Fifi sashayed along the wall. Her delicate features all seemed to smile in unison as her emerald eyes surveyed the scene. George and François gazed up at her, disciples before their goddess.

'You see, this little kitten-cat... ' – and George nodded at Dog, who was standing some way back from the wall so he wouldn't frighten Fifi – '... is in training. He has some deep issues that need addressing, with regards to demeanour and vocalisation, and doesn't mean to offend in any way. Fortunately, he is progressing well, so should become a most marvellous and dignified cat one day, all in good time.'

'I… I'm… very sorry,' said Dog to Fifi.

'I didn't mean to frighten you… I just couldn't help it. It's just that… 'Dog'… happens to be my name.'

'Miiiiiiooooooaaaaawwwww-prrrup-prrrup,' said Fifi with a little sideways nod of her head, and the tiniest flick of her sleek silky tail. This meant that Dog was forgiven, something for which he was enormously grateful.

Eric meanwhile was rolling in the nasturtiums, scratching a terrible itch on his back with the help of a very squashed and stunned worm.

George and François continued bickering over Fifi.

And Dog – well, Dog sat and wondered why all these cats seemed to go mad whenever the she-cat appeared.

One minute, George and François were the best of friends, behaving like the most decent and dignified cats. And the next they were arguing and squabbling like the most ill-behaved little kittens – and all because another cat had walked along the wall. It was most strange and confusing.

Suddenly, Fifi's ears pricked up, her beautiful black fur stood on end, and she hurtled along the wall in the direction of her two-legs' house.

George turned round and looked accusingly at Dog.

'What did you say, kitten-cat?' he snapped, 'Did you yap? Wag your tail?'

'Oh no,' said Dog, 'I… I don't think so, anyway… '

Then they heard it, even though it was some way off: the long low growl of a monstrous miaow, like something terrible and ancient come to life, crawling from the primaeval mud – something that was now on the prowl, and hungry on the hunt for prey.

A look of horror darkened George's face, and his ears twitched in nervous spasms.

'Come on, kitten-cat!' he ordered, 'We have to hide. Behind the shed – now!'

Dog didn't question why. He trusted George implicitly.

'Eric? François?' called George, but they had already scarpered – no doubt to seek out a safe and secret place, in which to skulk until the danger had passed.

Silence.

A stifling and eerie quiet descended on the garden. The birds had ceased tweeting and chirping in the trees, the wind had stilled to a stagnant hush, and the dead breath of a strange uncertain stillness sat stale and suffocating on the evening air.

Dog held his breath, just like he did when mousing. He could hear the drumming of his heart in his chest now that the usual hectic and noisy world of the garden had been transformed into a world of no noise at all.

The two cats crouched low behind the shed. George occasionally poked his ears and eyes above the old bucket and piles of wood that they were hiding behind, to try and hear and see what he knew was coming.

'What is it?' asked Dog, in the tiniest, most wispy whisper he could.

'Shhh!' said George, more quietly than Dog had heard him say anything else before. He put a paw over his mouth and gestured that the kitten-cat should do the same.

And then Dog heard the growl of a miaow again – much louder this time. It was a deep, low sound that had clearly been made by a very large and formidable animal indeed.

Dog stood next to George and poked his head up. And then he saw it – a huge grey tom prowling along the garden wall.

The cat was massive, a monster at least twice the size of any that Dog had ever seen before, both in terms of length and breadth – including George, and he was very well-padded indeed.

He was grey as rock – short-haired, with big broad shoulders and a solid muscle-packed frame. But it was his very *presence* that was huge, more than anything else, as though he had been carved out of some enormous craggy cliff and brought to life by unseen feline forces to rule the world.

His wide paws padded so softly that even Dog – a young kitten-cat with keen ears – struggled to hear anything at all. But he could see the claws alright, even at that distance – lethal sharp things, glinting there like shards of glass, waiting to be unsheathed and to inflict damage on whoever or whatever got in their way.

George and Dog watched the monstrous cat stop and sniff the air, the threat of confrontation daubed on his torn slab of a face. Then, in one sudden swift movement, he turned his terrifying head around to look, with eyes a dreadful yellow, to the place behind the shed where the cats were sitting.

Dog gasped – a short sharp intake of breath that was almost identical to the sound emitted from George at the self-same moment. The cats ducked down and lay as flat as they could on the ground. George hoped that they had not been seen – or, if they had, that the intruder would be well-fed already and in no mood to fight or bite.

It had been a while since George had seen this monstrous tom. He thought perhaps that he might have 'snuffed it' – but no such luck. He was clearly alive and well, though with some new scars cutting across the zigzags of the old ones on his face. Dog had never seen such markings on a cat before, and they made him look terrifying.

George lay on Dog, covering him like a blanket, just in case the monster investigated behind the shed. He was prepared to fight to protect the kitten-cat, to use his body as a shield to protect his charge from harm, as was his duty.

But, as it turned out, the tom did not appear. And when – several long breathless moments later – George poked his head up to look at his wall and garden, there was no sign of him at all. The monster was gone.

'Phew,' said George – and he meant it, 'Panic over, kitten.'

'But who… or… what… was that cat?' piped up Dog, his tongue poking out.

'That,' explained George, 'was *The Bruiser* – an exceedingly dangerous animal. If you ever see him, you must run for home as fast as possible. Is that understood?'

Dog thought for a moment.

'Is… *this* my home?' he asked, unsure.

'Why, of course it is, little kitten-cat,' said George, 'Until you find a two-legs and a home of your own.'

Dog was so delighted with this exciting news that he wagged his white-tipped tail as hard as he could and yapped, just like the silliest of puppies. His tongue was flopping out in the most inelegant un-feline manner too and this had the effect of facilitating some rather unsightly doggy-style dribbling.

George closed his eyes. He thought he had been

making good progress – and it was true that Dog's tail-wagging habit and dog noises had become noticeably less regular since his lessons had begun – but now he seemed right back to square one.

'Yap yap yap,' said Dog, 'Rrruffff-rrruffff-rrruuuffff!'

'Do you mind!' snapped George, 'Have you forgotten everything I have taught you, kitten-cat?'

'Yap-yap-yap-miiiiiaaaaaaooooowwwww!' said the kitten, his words fading to embarrassed silence as he realised his error. He sat down to think.

'Are you destined always to be a cat-dog dog-cat confused type of creature, and not the elegant dignified feline you could be – if only you made the effort to reach your full potential? Well, are you?'

George was raising his miaow-voice now and Dog didn't like it. His ears flattened against his sorrowful head, which he bowed down low in embarrassment and shame so that his nose almost touched the ground.

'I am disappointed, kitten-cat, most disappointed indeed!'

'I... I'm sorry,' said Dog, 'but... sometimes... I... just can't help doing the things I do... '

George tutted, then shook his head sadly. He put a comforting tom-paw on the kitten-cat's shoulder.

'It's not easy being a cat, kitten, not easy at all,' he sighed, 'But it'll come, with practice – if you work hard, every day.'

This, George knew, was what was called 'optimism'. The truth, however, was a great deal more pessimistic, because the old tom was no longer really convinced – if he ever had been – that teaching the kitten how to be a cat would achieve anything at all.

Maybe it was too late? Maybe too much damage had

been done? Maybe it was all impossible to repair and rectify?

But he had to try. Yes, George knew he had to at least *try* to change the kitten!

The pride of cats was at stake – and there was nothing he could think of that was more important than that.

'I'm doing my best, I really am,' miaowed Dog, almost in a whimper.

'I know, kitten-cat, I know,' and the old tom gave the kitten a little lick on the top of his head, just so he knew it too.

'Now,' said George, 'repeat after me: I am a cat.'

'I am a cat.'

'I am *not* a dog.'

'I am *not* a dog.'

'But a cat.'

'But a cat,' said Dog, proud as paws.

'Splendid!' miaowed George, 'Now I want you to repeat that nine times before each and every time you settle down to sleep. And before you wash. And at any time you think you may be about to wag your tail in happiness or make doggish noises, or when you find your tongue sticking out, puppy-fashion.'

'Why nine times?' asked Dog.

'Because it is better than eight times, and ten is rather overdoing it. Besides, we have nine lives, so nine is a good number of times to do anything really.'

This was an answer that made perfect sense to Dog.

'I am a cat,' he said, 'I am *not* a dog. But a cat!'

And he kept on mouthing the words as George led him into the kitchen for a well-earned pre-snooze snack.

Oh the horror! The almost un-miaowable horror that greeted the cats in the kitchen!

For George's bowl – the very receptacle that was never empty and which always contained sufficient food to nourish George (and sometimes his friends) at any time of day or night – was now sitting there on the mat, completely and utterly bare. The bottomless bowl did, indeed, have a bottom…

'Maybe she's forgotten to feed you?' said Dog, looking over at his mentor.

George surveyed the scene with a look of such hurt and sadness on his face that Dog was overwhelmed with anger at what The Lady had done. It was the duty of every two-legs to provide adequate food and water for cats – even the stupidest two-legs knew that, and there were already rather a lot of that sort about without The Lady becoming one of them too.

'When The Lady comes home, we should tell her!' suggested Dog, thinking about what Eric might do in such a situation, 'Complain loudly!'

'No,' muttered George in a low miaow, 'The Lady is not to blame. She has been taken over by a wrong 'un, that's all. She is not herself.'

'But I'm hungry,' said Dog, 'and you're hungry too!'

'I cannot deny it, kitten-cat… '

George's tummy was rumbling at the memory of better, well-fed days.

'However, hunger, though unpleasant, rarely proves fatal to felines with immediate effect.'

'But… '

'But… ' George went on, 'we need not go hungry, because there is always a way, if you look hard enough. That is the way of cats. Follow me.'

And so Dog followed George to the end of the garden, up onto the garden wall, along for quite a long way, past the neighbours' garden with its pond and trees, then down into the lane – then up onto another wall, then along a wall again, and along yet another wall, and down into a garden, and towards a big back door with a cat flap in it.

'Miiiiiaaaaaoooooowwwww,' called George in a whisper so quiet that Dog could barely hear it.

Suddenly, a rustling noise – and Fifi emerged from under a rubbery shrub.

'Miss Fifi,' said George, 'Please forgive us for disturbing you like this in such a sudden and intrusive manner. But disaster has struck, a catastrophe has ensued, and, for reasons yet unclear, we have no food to nourish us in our own home. It is for that reason that we humbly implore you that we may be allowed to partake of a snack in your two-legs' house.'

'Miiiiioooooaaaaawwwww-puurrrup-purrrrup-wiaow,' said Fifi, with a flick of the tail.

'Many thanks indeed,' said George, 'Say "thank you", kitten-cat.'

'Thank you, Miss Fifi,' said Dog – and, with that, Fifi disappeared back under the bush whence she had come.

George did not insist on her company. He well knew that she-cats enjoyed their privacy – (though he had no idea what they got up to for so long in their private places) – so he let Fifi leave without further ado.

'Come on, kitten-cat,' said George, stepping gingerly through the cat flap. Dog kept kitten-close behind.

In the kitchen, they gorged themselves on the big bowl of biscuits that Fifi's two-legs had left out for her, but they were sure to eat no more than half of what was there – which is the way any well-mannered cat should behave when invited to partake of another's rations.

Back in George's garden, and by now well-fed and satisfied, the two cats settled down for the night.

'And so ends another busy day,' yawned George, 'Tomorrow, kitten-cat, is another day – and the most splendid thing is, it always is… ' – and he curled up behind the shed, safe and warm and at home.

Dog washed his face as George had taught him, licking his paw at least three times, then wiping over his ear and face carefully until he was clean.

Then he curled up to sleep next to George who was, he knew, the best friend a kitten-cat like him could ever have.

CHAPTER 14

After his early morning patrol – a lengthy inspection of the garden and outlying territories (no problems to report, thank goodness!) – George returned home just as Dog was waking up.

'Good morning, kitten-cat,' he said, with an avuncular miaow.

'I think I… errr… overslept,' said Dog, yawning, 'Sorry.'

'Not to worry, kitten-cat, not to worry. *Never ever* apologise for sleeping. It is just not done. Apologising for such things is for working dogs and other imbeciles. We are above it.'

'Sorry… errr… I mean… I'm *not* sorry… I mean… yes, George,' said Dog, not sure what he meant.

'It's good that you are well-rested, kitten – we have an awful lot to get through today.'

Dog started his wash, just as George had shown him: paws, face, ears, chest, back, tail, tummy, bottom.

'Well done, kitten-cat. Splendid!' miaowed George, before turning to squint at the Spring sunshine. He took a deep fresh breath of the bright morning air.

'I instinctively feel that today is going to be *the* most marvellous and beautiful day,' he said.

On days such as this, George often woke The Lady with his enthusiastic singing. He was just about to go into the house to give his performance, when he heard a terrible noise.

It was a voice – the voice of The Man – and it was coming from the kitchen – *his* kitchen, where he went to get fed! He had assumed that The Lady had come home alone the day before – not with that Man two-legs again – but, oh how wrong he was!

His heart sank in his chest like a sack of drowning kittens as he realised that there would be no singing performance required that morning.

George peeped out from behind the shed to look through the kitchen window. There he was – The Man, the thief, the enemy – rushing to do something, knocking something over. This was a good sign, though – it meant that he was in a hurry and would leave soon. But his very presence there in the first place meant that he had stayed the night with The Lady.

How could she? thought George. How *could* she? With *him!!!*

There was only one rational explanation: The Man had brainwashed The Lady so much that she was now completely under his control and no longer in charge of her own mind. It happened sometimes with two-legs, most often when they were suffering from the thing they called 'love', a terrible affliction which makes them take complete leave of their senses.

Love, for two-legs, was like a very strong dose of catnip, but worse – much worse. It could last for many moons and summers too, though it usually disappeared as quickly and unexpectedly as it arrived, (a bit like diarrhoea or a bad case of wind), at which point things could happily return to normal.

But George, if pushed, had to admit he knew all about love too – about how, when a two-legs loves you and you love them, as it was between George and The Lady, nothing else seemed to matter – except for the treble pleasures of eating, sleeping and washing, of course (and when did they ever *not* matter?)

George's ear-tips trembled with yearning at the sound of The Lady's voice.

And then – *and then!* – he saw something so awful that his claws tensed up tight at the terrible sight: The Man *kissed* The Lady.

'Yeeeuuuukkkk!' said Dog, who had poked his head up to join his teacher gawping at the scene.

George was about to say that the kitten-cat had just taken the miaows out of his mouth, but knew that it would be dishonourable, disloyal and undignified to criticise his own two-legs in the presence of other cats. He would therefore keep his disgust to himself, though he couldn't help his ears wilting limp – a look, as all vigilant two-legs know, is only ever seen in cats if they are ill or hurt in some way.

Not long after, the front door slammed. George scrambled up onto the wall just in time to see The Man driving away in his wheel-box.

Interloper suitably expelled, George jumped down again into the garden.

'Stay here, kitten-cat!' he instructed, 'That's an order!' – and he trotted off in the direction of the house.

Dog miaowed and nodded his obedience, but not before George's tail had disappeared into the cat flap like a big ginger worm retreating into its burrow.

'Hello, boy!' greeted The Lady, when she saw him,

'And where've you been hiding then?'

But George was in no mood for idle cat-chat. He was here to protest – and this he did, as loudly as possible and in no uncertain terms.

'Miiiiiaaaaaooooowwwww-yowwwww-yowwwww-wahhhhh-mmmmmiaow-wowwwww-mmmmmiaow-wowwwww-yowwwww!'

'George!' said The Lady, bending down and stroking his head, 'Whatever's wrong?'

The old tom told her quite clearly and in some detail what was wrong – yet again. But he got the distinct feeling that The Lady wasn't listening – not properly, anyway. The Man had obviously managed to make her deaf when he brainwashed her – it was the only explanation for her complete inability to understand a single thing he was saying!

'Oh, don't be cross and grumpy, George,' said The Lady.

She knelt down to stroke and smooth his ginger back-fur, then picked him up and tickled him under his chin in her usual way.

But George was having none of it. He refused to purr, and would continue to do so until he managed to convince The Lady that The Man was a wrong 'un, and that she should, under no circumstances, invite him back into their home again.

'Be like that then,' said The Lady, putting George down, 'You always get in a huff when you're hungry, don't you, pussy cat?'

George protested loudly, but was rudely ignored. If only two-legs could understand how *infuriating* that was! Though he was delighted to hear The Lady opening some food for him – at long last. It had only taken her a whole long hungry night and day to notice that his bowl was empty!

George was about to miaow *'about time too!'*, but then hesitated. He would eat first and complain later – which seemed the best order by far.

'He's right, y'know, you are getting podgy – that's why we need to put you on a diet,' said The Lady, doling out a disgracefully inadequate amount of food into his bowl, 'It's for your own good, George – a cat your age…'

Now, the idea that a two-legs could decide what was for a cat's 'own good' was so absurd, insulting and demeaning that it didn't even merit a reply. So George instead gave The Lady a very hard stare, and let that be the end of it.

There was, needless to say, nothing *wrong* with his age. It was a good age, a mature age, an autumnal age of wisdom and reflection – and (The Lady please take note!) an age of hearty healthy appetites.

How was a cat to survive on such small rations? There was barely enough for a newly-weaned kitten in his bowl, and George was a mature and solid tom-cat – he had his needs. And he needed, above all, adequate servings of nutritious and delicious food – and plenty of it! How else was he supposed to get the energy to sleep and wash and patrol the garden?

And it was even worse because George knew that The Lady was aware of all this. She knew that he needed energy intake in the form of regular snacks, if he was to engage in energy expenditure.

Now, on these paltry rations, there was nothing else for it – he would have to up his energy conservation program, with more regular catnaps, as well as upping his daily sleep from his usual minimum sixteen hours a day.

'Hello!' said The Lady, 'and what's *your* name?'

'Miiiaaaooowww-purrrupppp!' wailed Dog,

weaving in between The Lady's ankles, and rubbing his head gently against them.

'I told you to stay outside!' snapped George, 'You have blatantly disregarded my instruction in the manner of the most ill-behaved kitten-cat!'

The Lady picked up the kitten, and held him close to her face for inspection. He wagged his tail in happiness and poked his little pink tongue out – looking as sweet, adorable and irresistible as it was possible for him to look. Dog knew his strategy was working when The Lady beamed wide at him with a warm and friendly smile.

She then put the kitten down, took out a saucer, placed it next to the old tom's bowl, and forked generous helpings of food onto both. George knew The Lady couldn't deprive him of rations for long – no matter how addled her weak two-legs' brain became. Animal cruelty was just not in her repertoire.

'There,' she said, 'Now eat up, boys… I'm going to be late for work… '

Dog smiled a miaow at George. He was not amused, but could only admire the kitten-cat's successful strategy in eliciting more rations from a two-legs – and in the exact manner that George had trained him, too! It meant that some of his lessons were getting through to his student, at least.

'Oh, one more thing,' said The Lady, 'Look!'

And she held down her hand to George who, despite being grateful for the feed, was still tetchy as a tick.

Why was The Lady holding her hand in his face? George had no idea. No matter how long he lived he would always be baffled by the strange and peculiar ways of two-legs.

'Do you like it?' she beamed, 'It's my engagement ring – from my fiancé. It means we're going to be married, though we're not sure when exactly.'

Now George had been given bad news on several occasions during his long and reasonably happy life – news of calamities and disasters, injuries and deaths of neighbours and friends, sadnesses and sorrows aplenty, and tribulations and trials that would have tested the most resilient of cats. But never ever in all his cat years had he heard something so terrible, so awful, so completely and utterly wrong as he heard that morning.

'Noooooooooooo!' he yelled in protest – which came out more like: 'Miiiiiaaaaaoooooowwwww-owww-owwww-yowww-yowww-hssssssss!'

But The Lady was not there to hear him. She had left the kitchen and was heading out of the house. The rattling slam of the front door confirmed her exit.

George slumped on the floor, paws tucked under his body, and just sat there, a solid square shape of well-proportioned ginger cattiness, watching Dog enjoying his breakfast. He just wasn't hungry any more – a highly unusual state of affairs for a feline; a unique state of affairs for George.

'Get a move on, kitten-cat!' grumped George, 'We need to start lessons as soon as possible.'

Dog said nothing. He didn't think he had ever been so hungry and quickly finished every scrap and morsel of food on the saucer (though he didn't touch George's bowl out of respect, even though the old tom had eaten no more than a mouthful or two from it himself).

'Yap-yap-yap,' said Dog when he'd finished, and started wagging his tail in joy at his tummy's fullness.

'I can see,' said George, a disapproving glare widening his eyes, 'that lessons in appropriate communication are called for.'

CHAPTER 15

'To miaow or not to miaow,' said George, 'that is the cat question. But, needless to say, on no account must any feline ever yap or bark or woof!'

Dog hung his head in shame at his indiscretions.

'I am a cat,' he chanted, 'Not a dog, but a cat!'

'Splendid!' said George, 'It never hurts to remind oneself of that most wonderful of facts. Well done.'

Dog's ears pricked up at the praise.

George seemed much more cheerful than he had been earlier on. He always became like this when he was teaching. It was almost as if he really enjoyed tutoring the kitten in the complexities of how to be a cat, though Dog imagined that it must be a real chore.

The kitten knew that his teacher would obviously much prefer to be engaged in the essential activities of eating, sleeping or washing really, as was his right as a mature and self-sufficient tom-cat of advancing years. So his generosity in giving his time and dedication to the teaching task was something to be appreciated at all times.

'Now, it is worth remembering,' George went on, 'that often non-communication is the best communication there is.'

Dog's whiskers drooped and he squinted his eyes at the paradox. Predictably, his tongue poked its pinkness out in a look of absolute and utter bafflement.

'Let me explain,' miaowed George, 'Imagine, if you will, that one of us – a cat or a kitten – has accidentally caused a breakage in the household, or perhaps eaten something that two-legs did not want us to eat – though we are assuming here that the usual rule applies and that it was the two-legs who were at fault for leaving the breakable object right where we wanted to walk, or in leaving food within reach of our paws – which everyone knows, makes it morally and logically ours by right.'

Dog nodded. He loved it when George managed to hit the mouse on the head just so. Everything he said seemed to make so much sense, it was really quite uncanny.

'In such a situation, silence is called for. Not a miaow, or a purrrrup, or even the teeniest of little squeaks is necessary. In fact, any such utterance could well make the situation worse. Remember, the two-legs may well be angry and fractious due to their loss, so must be approached with the greatest of care.'

Dog wasn't sure what 'fractious' meant, but it sounded right somehow, and he knew that angry two-legs were best avoided at all times – as were angry cats, for that matter.

'Remember, kitten-cat – if no-one saw you do it, then no-one can prove you did it. So you should not allow yourself to be interrogated – and you must not, in any circumstances, lie. A dignified silence will suffice. And if you wish, you may use *the look*, thus… '

On George's face, there bloomed an expression of exquisite and all-encompassing boredom – his gaze fixed serenely on the middle-distance, each eye glazed and distant, as if lost in a living and waking sleep.

'See?' said George, 'Now you try.'

Dog did so, but found that it was actually extremely tricky to get that gormless middle-distance stare just right. To his embarrassment, he became aware that he was making the face he often makes whenever he does a mess, and was shamed by the association (cats of all ages and stations in life prefer to keep such things as private and secret as possible, as the more perceptive of two-legs know).

'It'll come, kitten-cat, it'll come,' said George, observing Dog's struggle, 'Practice – that's all it takes. Right, moving on… '

Dog sat up straight. He was keen to learn all about cat communication, although he knew some of it already, as if it had always been there, somewhere in between his ears. But there was a lot he did not know too – sometimes more than he cared to think about.

George cleared his throat:

'Two-legs cannot purr. This is an exceedingly curious phenomenon, because they can make the strangest of noises, and plenty of them, at all pitches and volumes imaginable. But alas, no purr. An evolutionary error, no doubt – but as they lack the confidence and serenity necessary, hardly surprising. They are, after all, from a species that is almost furless, so cannot even puff themselves up to look bigger when in any confrontational situation. Instead they make the most awful shouting and yelling and screaming noises, and sometimes use their paws for fisticuffs and violence, occasionally even against cats.'

Dog gasped in shock. He was always saddened when he heard about two-legs hurting cats, but knew that it was true. He had seen with his own eyes how The Man had treated his mentor, flinging him into the garden like that – though he was pleased to see that George's limp had mostly gone by now.

'Of course, we cats can also make some quite hideous caterwauling noises, and the occasional plaintive wail when the need arises – and our habit of hissing needs no introduction. But today I would like to concentrate on the two main sounds in our repertoire – the miaow and the purr.'

'Miaow!' said Dog in the affirmative.

'Good! Now then, kitten-cat – the miaow. What it is and how to use it. We are indeed fortunate as a species that our miaow resembles, if only to ears less acutely tuned than our own, the sound of two-legs' kittens, which are called 'babies'. This is a fortuitous coincidence which we felines have learnt – through our shrewdness, skill and natural cunning – to exploit to its full potential over the long cat centuries.'

'*Ba-bies,*' said Dog, mouthing the word as if to taste it. He had never seen any two-legs' kittens, and wasn't sure he'd like to either – but was glad he now knew what they were called, just in case he ever met one.

'Now don't worry about them, kitten-cat. All we are interested in today is the sounds we make. There are several types of miaow, and a limited number can be understood by two-legs, especially if you teach them. For example, if you make the same miaow sound each time you want fresh food to be served, then your two-legs, no matter how slow and simple, will be able to associate that miaow sound with your desire for food, and thus serve your needs.'

Dog thought that this sounded highly efficient as well as completely fair – good communication was clearly as essential for two-legs as it was for cats.

'Most two-legs are capable of learning seven or eight sounds, and the most intelligent can manage a vocabulary of ten or more. Believe me, kitten-cat, this is more than adequate for our purposes. Of course, two-legs will typically always consider *themselves* intelligent for working out what you are saying, even after you have gone to the considerable effort of teaching them the vocabulary you want them to know in the first place! Forgive them their rudeness and ignorance – as an inferior species they really can't help it, you know. All noble and honourable cats must at least try to tolerate their many failings.'

Dog shook his head in disbelief. These two-legs did seem to be very primitive creatures indeed.

'By great good fortune,' said George, 'there are miaows for each and every occasion. There is the pitiful miaow, a plaintive wail best used when you are hard done by in some way – usually because your two-legs, in their cruel stupidity, are underfeeding you, either out of thoughtlessness or spite, perhaps as punishment for something which all logic says was their fault anyway! Be careful, however, not to be too self-pitying. Nobody likes a whinger! So use the pitiful miaow with great caution.'

Dog nodded and gave the most plaintive, pitiful miaowing wail that George had ever heard.

'I say, that's marvellous,' he said, 'You seem to have got that off to perfection.'

'*Purrrrrrfection,*' purred Dog, smiling with his whiskers.

'Kitten-cat, please,' said George, (who didn't like jokes), 'Purrs come later. For now, it's the miaow.'

'Miaow,' said Dog. He sat up straight and twitched his ears to learn.

'Jolly good,' said George, 'Now, one of the most effective miaows is the chirrup-miaow – if you listen to Miss Fifi, you will hear how well she produces this exquisite sound. Something like 'purrrrup-miaow', though I am by no means the best practitioner… '

'Purrrrup-miaow,' echoed Dog.

'Splendid!' said George, 'Now this sound has a most marvellous softening-up effect on two-legs. Remember – we cats are naturally graceful so we cannot fail to charm them into submission. The chirrup-miaow is the killer blow. Trust me.'

Dog would indeed trust George in this, and couldn't wait to try it out sometime on a two-legs – though, as he'd only just met The Lady, he thought he'd better not push it.

'There are many and varied varieties of miaow, voiced and unvoiced, loud and quiet, aggressive and calm. But perhaps the most effective of all is the silent miaow. If you really want to tug their heart-strings, to make two-legs feel guilty at how badly they are treating you, to drive home the point in a way that is really staggeringly effective, then the silent miaow is unquestionably the finest tactic known to cat. However, as with all of our greatest qualities, its power grows with expert and minimal usage. Overuse can weaken even the most effective miaow, noisy or silent.'

Dog nodded. It was all a lot to take in, but he would do his best.

'Observe,' said George. He then proceeded to look plaintively at Dog – (who was, for the purposes of the lesson, standing in as a two-legs) – before opening his mouth as if to miaow, but allowing no sound at all to issue forth from his lips. The effect was, quite simply, magical.

'Wow!' said Dog.

He was amazed at how something so simple could be so effective. George's silent miaow was even engendering sympathy and pity in his fellow feline, so one could only imagine what effect it would have on a two-legs!

'Now you try,' instructed George, ever-willing to let the little kitten-cat have a go at putting theory into practice.

Dog tried his best to look as plaintive as George had done. He opened his mouth for his silent miaow, not wanting or expecting to make a sound, but a tiny thin squeaky miaow emerged as if all by itself anyway. Dog tutted in frustration.

'Ah now, you see, that's very common.'

'Yap-yap-yap,' said Dog, annoyed at himself.

'But *that*, kitten-cat, is not very common at all.'

'Sorry,' miaowed Dog, 'it just… came out… the squeaky miaow… and the yap… '

'Never mind,' said George, 'Chin up! You'll get the hang of it in the end. And now we shall consider the purr – which falls, rather neatly into two distinct categories – the anticipatory purr and the thankful purr.'

Dog had no idea whatsoever what 'anticipatory' meant, but thought it might have something to do with ants, of the type that sometimes walk all over your fur and itch you when you're asleep. This sounded very odd indeed and nothing much to do with purring.

George soon corrected the misapprehension:

'The *anticipatory* purr is the less common of the two. It is the sound you should make when your two-legs comes home from hunting with their shopping, and is usually used to whet the appetite and thank two-legs in anticipation of fare to be proffered.'

Dog stuck his tongue out in confusion. His pointy ears wilted limp with the weight of unfamiliar words. George noticed his lack of comprehension. Some clarification was called for:

'To thank them for food in *advance*, in other miaows,' he said.

'Oh, I *see*,' said Dog, 'thank you.'

Anticipatory was yet another word to add to his burgeoning new collection.

'But much more common, and used a great deal in some households, is the purr of thanks. Two-legs are extremely vain creatures, and simply lap up flattery as we would cream, so they should always be thanked when they do their duty. We cats never expect such thanks, but we have to accept our role as the superior species here and should not resent the greater praise that two-legs receive for doing so very little to what, I am sad to say, is often a barely adequate standard.'

It all seemed very unfair to Dog, but he was prepared to accept the way things were and integrate fully into cat society. It was, he knew, the only way he was ever going to really fit in and find a two-legs of his own to look after.

'In addition to all these,' said George, 'there is the eating purr – a sub-category of the thankful purr really

– which is not uncommon. It is permitted for a well-mannered cat to purr whilst eating a particularly delicious morsel as a treat. Indeed, it is encouraged and serves the double purpose of saying 'thank you' to your two-legs, and also reminding them that you find this particular type of food – roast chicken, say – especially delicious.'

Dog put his paw up.

'Does it have to be roast chicken?' he asked.

'Certainly not. Roast chicken just happens to be my own particular preference, kitten-cat; you may well have another. We cats are all different in our tastes.'

Actually, Dog didn't know, because he didn't know too much about other cats. But he decided not to say anything because George was clearly on a roll.

'Anyway,' continued George, 'all two-legs know that a purr is the most wonderful thank you that we can give them. They positively marvel at our ability to purr at so many levels. From the tiniest barely audible whisper – useful to making them wonder if their behaviour has been accepted, to the loudest, most magnificent, most thunderous leonine purr, of such a volume that it can even be heard in adjoining rooms. Every cat is perfectly free to make such purrs when he sits absolutely secure and happy in his two-legs' arms.'

Dog started purring at this point, beginning with the littlest of purrs, and steadily increasing the volume until his voice was as loud as he could make it. This was not very loud, it's true – but it would grow as he grew, George assured him, until it equalled that of any other cat.

'You can of course rub or nudge your head or neck against a two-legs at this point – against an arm, a chin or a cheek. The choice is yours. Two-legs show affection by stroking and grooming us, of course, which makes us purr even louder because we understand, even if they may not, that it is usually the inferior animal which grooms the superior. At this point, a lick may be given, to the hand or even the face – but be very careful not to get carried away and bite, or at least to do so with tender care, as if holding a kitten by the scruff of the neck. *Gently does it* should be the guidance here.'

Dog delicately licked a front paw and gave it a little bite to show he had understood.

'Splendid!' said George, 'And remember, there is also our usual fail-safe padding manoeuvre, whereby we knead two-legs' flesh with our paws, and sometimes even with our claws, though we must at all times remember just how sharp they can be – and just how absurdly thin two-legs skin is too. This kneading also serves to spread our scent throughout our home territories, especially in our favourite spots. It is of course what we did as kittens to both thank our motherly milk-givers and to better encourage flow from their teats… '

'Did some cat mention teats?' said Eric, who had appeared on the wall and was watching George and Dog's noisy lesson in the sun, 'Cor blimey, what a racket! I ain't never 'eard such a rumpus!'

CHAPTER 16

'Eric, we are in the middle of a lesson here.'

'What's it on? Teats?'

'Most certainly not!'

'Shame,' wailed Eric, 'If there's one lesson every little tom-cat should 'ave, it's the one on teats… '

'Now look… ' said George.

'I've been learning all about miaows and purrs,' said Dog, proud as paws.

He liked Eric, even though he knew he could be terribly naughty at times and wind George up something rotten.

'Miaows and purrs eh?' said Eric, jumping down off the wall into the nasturtium bed.

He rolled over in one slick gymnastic motion to land standing on all four feet facing Dog.

'So George, when yer gonna start teaching the kitten all about the special noises what we cats make – the caterwauling and crying we do when we's out on the prowl? When a tom-cat and a she-cat… '

'Eric, puuuurrrrlease!' said George, 'The kitten-cat is far too young for such things. His learning is a most serious and important matter. It should be a rounded and full education which will allow him to live the dignified life of a respectable and noble cat. It should not be smutty.'

'And where d'you fink you came from, eh? Under a catnip bush?'

Eric rolled over convulsed with laughter. Dog couldn't help giggling too, but was immediately silent when George gave him a very hard stare indeed.

'Not in front of the kitten, Eric, please!' he said, sternly.

'Oh, it's alright,' said Dog, 'I already know everything about sex. I've watched cats and dogs doing it so many times now that it's all getting very boring actually.'

Both Eric and George sat and stared open-mouthed at Dog, who had no idea why these mature tom-cats would think he was as ignorant as a little mewling kitten. He was one summer old, after all – and would be a grown-up cat by the end of the summer that would soon be here. And there they were, treating him like a blind little new-born!

Eventually, Eric spoke:

'So, kitten-cat, what d'yer fink of yer course so far eh? Is old George learnin' you how to be a good 'n' proper cat?'

'Oh… I… I haven't thought about it very much,' said Dog.

'Stuff and nonsense!' miaowed George, 'Every cat *thinks*, even a little kitten-cat like you. That is what separates us from the lower animals – I need hardly mention that canines are not known for their thinking skills.'

Dog and Eric nodded at each other at the accuracy of this observation which, although rather obvious, was one that was always worth repeating

'You are a kitten-cat,' said George, 'therefore, you are thinking all the time, whether you realise it or not. You're just not *thinking* about what you're thinking.'

'Oh,' said Dog, 'Maybe that's it… '

He didn't sound very convinced.

'Course it is!' miaowed Eric, 'It's as plain as the whiskers on yer furry face!'

'How else would you be able to talk, kitten-cat, if you were not thinking, hmmm?' said George to his charge.

But it was François, newly arrived on the wall, who answered:

'Ah oui, mon ami,' he said, his words dripping with wisdom, 'but zere are a lot of two-legs who do not sink very much at all but who always do most of zer talking, non?'

The old tom thought for a moment and twitched his white whiskers. He really didn't approve of interruptions to the lesson, but on the other paw he certainly had to admit that François had a point.

'Ah yes,' said George, 'but this little kitten-cat is not a two-legs.'

'Ah oui,' said François, 'he eez not. He eez zer cat who sinks he eez zer dog, n'est-ce pas?'

'He has some… issues… yes… but nothing we cannot rectify with hard work, perseverance and regular practice. The kitten-cat is young. He can learn.'

'I am a cat,' said Dog, walking to and fro along the garden path, 'Not a dog – but a cat… '

'You see?' said George, 'And look at his tail – up high in the air without so much as a hint of a wag.'

Eric and François watched Dog parade back and forth on what could only be called his very own cat-walk.

'I have taught him all about posture – in our series of lessons entitled *The Tail: what to do with it, where it goes, and how to maintain it.* So the kitten-cat now knows to keep his tail up at all times when walking along, to flick it if he's not satisfied with food or servings, to tuck it under when he's sleeping, and only to wag it when he is irritated or cross.'

'Ah oui,' said François, 'zer tail eez so important, mon petit – zer tail eez zer mirror of zer mind, non?'

'Quite so,' said George, 'Make a note of that, kitten-cat, so you don't forget.'

'*The tail is the mirror of the mind,*' chanted Dog, an echo of truth on the wind.

'By my paws, indeed it is,' said George, 'and it is only through regular and conscientious practice that you will be able to discover the wide range of emotions it is capable of displaying – which are, incidentally, far greater than those which may be communicated by contortions of the face.'

'Like this!' said Eric, sticking his tongue out, bending his ears back and making his eyes pop out to create a grotesque gargoyle of a face he always used to make kittens giggle.

Dog laughed; George didn't; François looked serious.

'Georges,' said François, 'I sink somesing, it 'as upset you. I aff 'eard zat zer Lady is *engag-ed.*'

'How did you know?' asked George, head hung low.

'How we know what we are know must to be kept un grand secret, Georges. Mais la question, c'est ça: what eez eet zat we must to do, maintenant?'

'Ah, now, I am glad you mentioned that,' said George, 'because – I have a plan.'

'What, anuvver one?' giggled Eric, rolling on a snail.

George ignored him. The snail couldn't, but was lucky that the stray's long matted fur created a cushioning effect which prevented any catastrophic breakage. It was a lucky escape.

'I have been thinking hard about the predicament which has presented itself,' said George, 'And ever since this morning when The Man's takeover of the household was confirmed, and The Lady showed me the shiny thing on her finger, I have come to a very clear conclusion – and a very definite decision.'

'Cor blimey, 'bout time too,' scoffed Eric, his face poking out from the nasturtium flowers, 'Bring out the biscuits!'

George stood up straight, cleared his throat with a little cough, then said – in the slow low tones of gracious gravitas, like the king of all cats:

'Something must be done!'

Silence. The miaowed words hung heavy as sky water clouds in the air.

Eventually, Eric spoke:

'Thassit?' he said, 'That's the plan?'

'Well… '

'Get real, guv'nor! You're 'avin' a laugh!'

'Sacrebleu, Georges,' said François, 'Zut alors! Ziss eez not zer plan, ziss eez seulement zer *intention*.'

'I have been rather busy teaching the kitten-cat, you know… Besides, it never pays to rush these things. I've been thinking… and thinking deeply… It takes a lot of time to think, more time than *some* cats can possibly imagine,' the old tom miaowed, glaring somewhat cattily at Eric.

Dog felt a pang of guilt flutter through his fur. If it wasn't for his presence, George would have had more time to think and come up with a plan to save The Lady. He was just about to say that he would do anything to help, and that perhaps the number of lessons could be reduced to free up some thinking time, when François beat him to it.

'Georges,' he said, 'zere eez one sing zat I am not telling to you before, about what zer Man 'as said... '

'Oh?' said George, ears pricking up.

'Ah oui. Zer Man he has steal zer shiny sings and put zem in zer pocket... '

'You's already told us that, mate,' said Eric.

'Ah oui, bien sur,' said François, 'But I was not telling to you zat zer Man he 'as also told to zer uzzer two-legs using zer sing he has hold to his ear, not only about zer 'rich pickings' and zer shiny sings – but also about what eez his plan... '

'Plan?' said George, 'What plan?'

'He has said zat his plan eez to marry zer Lady... '

'We know that. The poor Lady – a terrible case of brainwashing,' muttered George.

'Ah, but zere eez more.'

'More?'

'Mais oui. Zer Man he has told zat he want to marry zer Lady, zen to take all of her sings, and also to 'ave her 'ouse for to sell, so he will to get half of zer money – and zen he shall to leave zer Lady, toute seule, alone completely, and wizzout zer shiny sings or zee 'ouse, and wiz nussink at all. Zut alors!'

'The brute!' yelled George, the tips of his ears trembling with a very feline form of indignation.

'Bloomin' 'eck!' said Eric, 'That Man two-legs really *is* a wrong 'un – even worse than all the uvver two-legs, an all!'

'By my paws!' miaowed the old tom, and he stretched his claws in and out at the thought of The Man's dastardly plan.

Dog gave an unpleasant growl – which, as every cat who heard it had to admit inwardly, was rather too doggish for their liking.

'So I sink,' said François, 'zat you have zer need for zer plan, Georges, and quickly if you please – because zer Lady she eez in zer danger most terrible!'

George could not disagree. The situation was urgent and The Lady was in great peril. That is why he needed to think. And that is why he needed to sleep – so he went behind the shed, curled up into a tight fluffy ball and closed his eyes.

Dog followed suit, and Eric and François found their own places in the garden for a much-needed nap as well. It was time to *let sleeping cats lie*.

Soon, they were all fast asleep and – despite appearances to the contrary – thinking *very* deeply indeed.

CHAPTER 17

Dog was climbing a tree.

He had been woken early by the loudest two-wings' tweeting he had ever heard. So, though George was still snoring, he decided to get up and take a look. He could tell the tweeting was coming from the neighbours' garden, so jumped onto the wall and went to investigate.

And then he saw it. Up in the tall towering tree that stood in the next-door garden, there were more birds than he had ever seen before in his whole little life. His lower jaw instinctively trembled at the sight, and he made the 'nyatt-nyatt-nyatt' sound cats always make whenever they look up at two-wings or hear their noisy voices coming from the sky.

Every branch of the tree was lined with birds – every twig and stick of it was bending and buckling under their enormous collective weight.

Dog's eyes peered higher and higher up into the tree until he couldn't really see anything but a vast blur of birds, tweeting and squawking and chirruping up in the branches.

They were of all shapes and sizes and colours, and were no doubt out in the late Spring sunshine to attend some strange birdy meeting. Or maybe to make friends?

Birds always seemed to stick together that way, always needing to travel in flocks, unlike cats who liked to walk alone, even if they did enjoy company. Perhaps they were more like dogs who always wanted to be in packs – but of course canines couldn't fly (though some, no doubt, had tried and failed rather badly...)

'The dogs of the sky! Sky-dogs! Yap yap yap!' the kitten-cat said excitedly, clambering up the vertical tree trunk.

All he wanted was just one little bird in his mouth. Then he would take it home as a present for George who would be simply delighted – he so needed cheering up after all that had happened.

And George could give the bird to The Lady as a present – or, if he wanted, he could play with it and torture it for fun, then maybe eat it all by himself afterwards. Dog knew just how hungry George was for much of the time these days.

Dog climbed up into the branches, higher and higher and higher. The birds abandoned the branches and took flight as he approached.

Once, he lashed out his claws and skimmed the feathers of a little yellow-breasted bird, but it escaped and flew off into the big blue air, laughing at him, just like two-wings always do.

He knew he had to be careful. Birds had sharp beaks on their noses, and claws on their paws too which could do a cat some real damage.

Dog had been told this by George who said they always go for the eyes, but are usually no trouble, except when they have their downy kittens in their nests. Then they can be as vicious as anything, he said, though they didn't just pick on cats. They would also attack dogs and two-legs who went near sometimes – which seemed fair enough, all things considered.

Up, up, up went Dog, into the tree.

The birds on the branches went flying off screaming and squawking with mocking laughter. Soon the air was thick with wings, whizzing this way and that, an awful feathery swarm fluttering and flapping around him.

Then Dog stopped. He had been climbing for a long time and wasn't sure how high he was now.

So, taking a deep breath, Dog turned his head to the side and looked down. What Dog saw made his fur shudder to its roots.

Oh! My! Paws!

The ground below seemed to be ever so far away, so much so that the gardens and the walls and the houses looked like little toy miniatures at the end of a long dark tree-trunk.

It was only now that Dog thought about how he might get down from the tree. It was a serious oversight, but this thought simply hadn't occurred to him until then, despite his being taught on several occasions exactly what curiosity had done to the infamous proverbial cat.

'Miaow-wiaow-wiaow!' wailed the kitten, perhaps more in hope than expectation, in the most plaintive cry of self-pity his little mouth had ever emitted.

But no-one heard, because there was no other cat there, and no two-legs either – just Dog the cat and thousands upon thousands of twittering birds.

And then it started:

'Yeow!' yapped Dog as one of the bigger birds dive-bombed him and pecked him hard on the head.

'Yeow yeow yeow!' he yelled again as more and

more birds, of all shapes and sizes, did the same thing, jabbing their bony beaks into his body.

Dog knew he had to get down – and quick. But he had never gone down a tree this tall before. In fact, he had never gone *up* a tree this tall before either, which was a coincidence as predictable as it was unfortunate.

Slowly, and carefully, Dog began walking backwards down the tree trunk – a terribly tricky and difficult manoeuvre, as all cats know.

Walking backwards was bad enough. Dog remembered the time he met George and how he, a clever and highly experienced cat, had fallen off the wall while doing it. But walking backwards down a vertical tree trunk was, quite possibly, the worst manoeuvre known to cat, and Dog was attempting it all whilst being attacked by a swarm of two-wings too!

Faster and faster down the tree trunk Dog scrambled, his claws getting stuck in the bark and his balance all wrong. His white-tipped tail was of no help to him now…

And all the while the two-wings kept dive-bombing him even though he was in retreat (which was very rude and cowardly behaviour indeed, Dog thought).

And then, the inevitable. After one enormous dive-bomb by a very nasty-looking seagull with an orangey-yellow beak and black beady eyes like pebbles, Dog lost his footing. His front claws became detached from the tree trunk, making him fall backwards, and then he lost the grip with his back claws too, so that – within a couple of cat seconds – none of his four paws remained attached to the tree at all.

And so it was that Dog found himself falling through the air, completely unclawed and unsecured, plummeting to earth at speed.

Down he fell, not knowing when his fall would come to an end, and trying not to think too hard about what would happen when it did.

Down, down, down he went. Down to the ground. Down to his certain doom.

Dog kept his eyes shut fast. It was doubtful that any cat could land on all four feet from a fall like this and at this velocity, no matter what they said.

Cats may well be marvellously resourceful and creative creatures, but they are not super-felines with miraculous powers. There are, sadly, limits to even their enormous talents.

But, as George had taught him, there was always a chance of survival for cats who can grasp opportunities. So as he fell Dog kept trying to grab on to something, lashing out his claws in the hope that one would snag and catch hold of a branch, or even a twig, which might break his fall.

However, his claws made contact with nothing but endless empty air. So he continued plummeting to earth, the mocking noise of birdy tweeting squawking the sad soundtrack to his demise.

Dog squeezed shut his eyes and prepared for what would surely be a very hard and painful landing indeed – and quite possibly his last.

But – Dog was surprised to find – the landing never came. Oddly, the ground below him seemed to have vanished.

Surely someone couldn't have taken it away? Or maybe some two-legs had dug a hole and he was now falling into that? Two-legs dug a lot of holes, he knew – (he had seen them, in gardens and lanes and streets) – but surely even they couldn't have managed to dig that quickly, not even with the big wheel-boxes they use?

Slowly, Dog opened an eye, and then another, and he was amazed to find himself not plummeting to earth any longer, but floating up high in the big blue sky.

He was, he was stunned to discover, doing what the two-wings do.

He was, incredibly, flying!

Dog looked down at his paws and claws, scrambling away where he hung suspended in flight above the Earth.

That was it!

The grabbing and lashing out he had been doing to try and catch hold of a branch or twig must have made his paws become some sort of catty wings – though he didn't think what he was doing could reasonably be called flying in any way, shape or form. It was more like sky-walking really. And as Dog climbed higher and higher, the birds flapping around him certainly weren't laughing any more.

No – they were clearly worried and had a look of blind terror in their beady side-eyes as they witnessed the worst of their nightmares come to pass – a flying cat swooping this way and that, trying to catch them! They were fast, it's true, these two-wings, as they zigzagged and slalomed through the clouds, never bumping into each other, no matter how fast they flew – something Dog found particularly impressive.

Dog knew he wouldn't be able to catch a big two-wings, or one of the really fast ones, but the birdy kittens were a different matter. They were slower, less experienced, and they had not yet learnt how to use their developing wings to full effect. Or perhaps one of the older stragglers would be good place to start?

There was one two-wings in particular – a plump

specimen, with browny-orangey feathers, who looked a bit old and past it. He seemed fatter and slower than the rest – which made him the perfect target.

Dog well knew that, when faced with a 'safety in numbers' scenario, it was important for a predator to single out just one individual as quarry. It was so easy to get distracted by numbers – that's why mice, voles and similar species often played this trick. So all felines had to do their best to focus their thoughts and eyes in such circumstances, and shut out all but the target of their hunting desires.

The fat little bird flapped its wings, harder and harder and harder, but Dog was definitely gaining on him, getting closer and closer and closer, with each little paddle of his paws.

Down, down, down flew the bird – perfect, the kitten realised, for his very own dive-bomb.

So Dog stopped moving his paws and claws, and instead drew them in flat against his body. He pointed his nose and ears at the fat little bird below him, turning himself into a streamlined black-and-white arrow of a cat, and aimed.

Get ready. Set. Fire!

Dog plummeted towards the little bird, faster and faster – so fast that his little black ears were pushed flat against his head with the force, and a rushing wind blew into his eyes, making it hard to see.

Down, down, down he fell, closer and closer and closer to his target – and then the fat little bird turned round.

'Impossible!' thought Dog, 'It can't be!'

For there before him was a ginger-coloured bird with a face that bore the unmistakeable features of a cat called George.

'Nooooo!' yelled Dog, desperately trying to stop his dive-bombing. He had to back-paddle somehow! 'Nooooo!'

But the fat little bird just hung there in the air, flapping its podgy wings forlornly, looking breathless and sad, waiting for the flying cat to swoop down, snatch it in those merciless jaws and eat it all up. Waiting for the end…

'Nooooo!' screamed Dog, hurtling to earth, flapping his wing-paws frantically.

But he was unable to reverse his dive-bombing downward direction.

And the fat little bird and the ground below him were getting closer and closer and closer…

And then…

'Kitten-cat! Kitten-cat, *please!*' miaowed George.

Dog blinked open his eyes. He was sitting on top of George behind the shed, all four paws lashing this way and that, desperately clawing the air to try and get a paw-hold.

When Dog could see that it had all been a bad dream, he stopped paddling his paws, clambered down off George, and collapsed exhausted on the ground.

'I dreamt… I dreamt… something awful… something just so terrible…

'Shhh, little kitten-cat,' said George, offering a gentle paw of reassurance, 'It was just a nightmare – we all have them, especially in times of stress.'

Dog hung his head in shame and confusion. He was so glad to be back to reality – so relieved that the bad dream was over – but so embarrassed too that he had ruffled and messed up George's beautiful ginger fur.

'I'm sorry… ' he miaowed.

'No real harm done,' said George, deciding to ignore the puppyish tongue-poking for now.

He flattened his own fur slickly and neatly back in place, before giving Dog's head a couple of little licks of assurance and comfort.

'By great good fortune, it's almost time to get up anyway, so I should be thanking you really for waking me, kitten-cat.'

'Really?' said Dog.

It was a rare occasion indeed when a cat actually liked to be disturbed when busy with the business of sleeping.

'Oh yes,' said George, 'you see, I have a plan!'

CHAPTER 18

Later that day, everything was ready.

George had explained the plan of action to Dog several times, and also to Eric and François, who had kindly offered to help in any way they could. All they needed to do now was wait for The Lady to arrive back home with The Man. He would, they all knew, step into the garden to have a 'smoke-stick'. This was when they would strike.

The plan was simple.

George was to jump up at The Man's pockets, making sure he fished out the shiny things with his claws. At the same time, Eric would jump from the wall onto The Man's back and bite his neck, taking his attention away from what the old tom was doing. François would then stick his needle-sharp claws into The Man's shins and ankles, thereby flooring him: they would not let this wrong 'un run away, no matter what.

And Dog, being a little kitten-cat, so not well suited to the rough and tumble, would pick up some of the shiny things that George has fished out of The Man's pocket. He would then drop them at the feet of The Lady who would naturally have come outside because of all the commotion. She would consequently be able to see, in the evidence before her, that The Man was a common and controlling thief – and one who intended to bring her nothing but sorrow and harm.

The plan, even if George said so himself, was practically perfect. If The Man came back with The Lady that day – (which he would) – and if he stepped outside to have a 'smoke-stick' – (which he always did) – then nothing could possibly go wrong.

Or so the cats thought...

But something did go wrong – it went very wrong indeed.

And the reason for this disaster?

In a word: *catnip.*

The Man may well have been a wrong 'un – a wicked and devious thief and crook – but he was also rather bright, for a two-legs. He had obviously thought things through and was prepared. This was something George had failed to take into consideration: he was not, it seems, the only one who had a plan.

The cats waited for their moment, and then it came.

The Lady returned home, as planned.

She was with The Man, as planned.

The Man opened the back door and went for a smoke in the garden, as planned.

But then, the fatal fly in the saucer of cream – The Man walked into the garden and placed two small pots of catnip plants right under George's nose.

Now, all's *fur* in love and war, as everyone knows – but this really was below the waistline. It was, indeed, a veritable body blow right in the furry trousers and decidedly under the tail.

As soon as The Man put the pots of catnip under George's nose, the battle was lost – for, as all felines know, catnip contains a narcotic so strong that it can even lay low the largest of lions. So what chance did domestic cats have?

Within moments, George was rolling on the ground rubbing his fur obsessively against the pungent plants, pawing them, licking them, biting them, chewing them – and making a strange and ecstatic purring miaow sound which was certainly not at all like anything he had been teaching the kitten-cat in lessons.

The Man chuckled a nasty sneer at the intoxicated tom.

'That shut you up, didn't it, you stupid cat?!'

And, with that, The Man turned and started walking back into the house – at the very moment, by cruel coincidence, that Eric, (who had been lying low on the shed roof), decided to launch himself at his back.

Now, it was a long way down to the ground, especially from the shed roof, as Eric discovered when he missed The Man completely and crashed down into a flowerbed. This, together with two unfortunate snails and three squidgy worms, broke his fall, preventing serious injury, though he was rather stunned.

He got to his paws a little woozily, staggered over to the catnip and took a long and pain-alleviating sniff. Soon, he was in the same dazed elated state as George, rolling on the ground giggling like a kitten. Whenever he tried to stand up, he couldn't. He just kept flopping over and giggling at nothing and anything – worms, snails, nasturtiums, the wall, the sky, the air, his paws, and even his own tail…

François too succumbed. Seeing George so disarmed and disabled he had come out to help, but was soon as intoxicated as the others, even though he had tasted and sniffed plenty of pungent herbs and spices on his travels. This was, he would later conclude, a particularly strong variety of catnip. One sniff of it and all his strength suddenly left him, leaving him limp as a lettuce – or 'une salade' as he would have said if he'd been in the slightest bit coherent.

Only Dog was sober. He watched in horror from behind the shed the spectacle of three mature cats, including the highly respectable and upright George, rolling around in the flowerbeds and making the strangest noises. The Man was in the kitchen now, but Dog could still hear his words through the cat flap:

'There's three of 'em there now – damn strays, not just your old ginger, all rolling around like rats. You should call the council… '

'We're going to be *late*… ' called The Lady, opening the front door.

'Next time it'll be rat poison!' jeered The Man through the window.

But apart from Dog, the cats weren't listening. They were staggering around in the flowerbeds, completely oblivious to the danger they were in.

The Man was just about to open the back door again, when The Lady shouted:

'Come on! We have to leave *now!*'

Reluctantly, The Man turned away from the scene and left the kitchen. Something told Dog that if The Lady hadn't called at that moment then The Man might well have been out in the garden with a broom or a stick, and might well have inflicted some severe damage on the over-stimulated cats lolling around clumsy as puppies in the garden. It had been a lucky escape.

Dog had to put a stop to this. But how?

If he went anywhere near the catnip, he would clearly be affected too, and act all silly and wobbly like the grown-up cats around him. He had seen behaviour like this before – not in cats, but in two-legs, who seemed to behave in an infantile fashion and stagger around making silly noises whenever they drank certain liquids (this behaviour would not happen of course if they stuck to water and milk products as the superior feline species did).

It was while Dog was thinking about what he could do to help the situation that he turned towards a weed growing next to the shed, upon which was crawling a very slow and slimy snail. It was a Eureka moment!

In a flash, Dog lifted up the snail gently in his jaws, then used his paws to manoeuvre it in position over his nostrils. He held it there for a moment until its sticky foot became affixed to his face – which was uncomfortable, and slimy, and somewhat dirty, but Dog knew that sacrifices had to be made in such emergencies. When his nostrils were completely sealed to the air, he took a deep breath through his mouth and held it.

Then he walked forward, being careful not to dislodge the snail, grabbed the rim of one of the catnip plant pots with his teeth and dragged it gradually towards the place in the garden where two large dustbins stood. He returned and did the same with the other pot.

The effects of the catnip were still making the cats roll around on the ground. Eric and François were even singing something, though the miaows and the music were far too slurred for any of it to make sense.

After he had put the catnip pots well out of the way, Dog returned to the safety of the shed, where he gently pawed the snail off his nose and placed it back by the weed.

'Thank you,' he said, but the snail said nothing.

He's probably just in shock, thought Dog – but so would he be if some big creature had picked him up and used him as a nose-peg.

While Dog was waiting for the effects of the catnip to wear off, and for George, Eric and François to get back to normal, he gave himself a wash. It was just about the most thorough and careful licking he had ever given himself too: it is really not the easiest task to clean snail slime off a kitten's nose!

Eventually, the singing died down. When Dog poked his head from behind the shed, he could see that the cats were no longer rendered incomprehensible and babbling by the catnip. Instead, they seemed quiet and subdued, with heads hanging down in a way that signified either a headache, or shame, or quite possibly both.

George got up from where he lay and limped towards the back of the shed, where he curled up in a tight ball and closed his eyes. He said nothing.

François was silent too, as his eyes – and the mind behind them – slowly came back into focus. He walked to the end of the garden, jumped up onto the wall – (a bit unsteadily, it has to be said) – and was gone.

Only Eric spoke, beckoning Dog to come over and join him. He kept his miaow voice very quiet indeed, no doubt not to disturb George or alert other cats to the defeat and humiliation suffered by them all.

'Now what you seen weren't fair, kitten-cat,' said Eric, 'Well out of order, it was, and somefink only the worst of two-legs could even fink o' doin' to innocent cats.'

'It was that… plant,' said Dog, 'It made you all… silly… '

'That Man two-legs, he's clever – oh yes – much more *cleverer* than what most two-legs is. But then, 'ow was we s'posed to know he'd clobber us wiv catnip?'

'*Cat-nip?*' repeated Dog, 'Is that its name?'

'The very fella,' said Eric, 'But it's a very dangerous drug in the wrong paws, so don't you go tryin' it, kitten.'

'No, I won't,' said Dog, who wouldn't want to, not after seeing how strangely and stupidly the other cats behaved under the influence.

'Now, y'see, us cats what is experienced, like, can 'ave a good old sniff, enjoy ourselves, tickle our paws and whiskers, and then walk away. Not like them two-legs, what ain't never gonna know when to stop when they gets all *intoxificated…* '

Dog listened to this, but had to admit to himself that he hadn't seen any of the cats walk away after sniffing the catnip earlier. Stumbling and rolling around – falling over and staggering about and giggling at their own paws and tails, yes – but definitely no walking away.

'Except 'course wiv the really full-on strong varieties, like what was put out for us today,' explained Eric, 'Not even big wild jungle cats could cope wiv somefink strong as that… So don't you ever go 'avin' a sniff o' that whiff, kitten-cat, you hear me?'

Dog gave his head a little firm shake, then a nod, then another shake, which seemed to cover it.

'Maybe,' whispered Eric, with a wink, 'It's better not to, like, mention anyfink about this to any uvver cats, not for a good long while anyway, eh?'

'Oh no, of course not,' miaowed Dog.

'It's been a *knackerifying* day, all in all,' said Eric, jumping on the wall, 'and we all needs a good long rest to *recoverate* our strength.'

'Oh yes,' said Dog, 'George was looking very... tired... when he went for a sleep'

'I 'spect he looked as weak as a kitten – no offence, like.'

Eric looked over to where George lay behind the shed.

'Look after him, kitten-cat, eh?'

'I will,' said Dog, 'always.'

'And kitten?' called Eric, loping off towards the end of the wall.

'Yes?' miaowed Dog.

'Fanks, y'know, for everyfink – the snail, the nose, for taking that... stuff away from us... '

'Oh, I just did what I could,' said Dog, giving a happy little wag of his white-tipped tail at the compliment.

'You done good, kitten-cat – you done well good. But there ain't gonna be no bringin' out the biscuits today, more's the pity... '

And with that, and a one-eyed farewell wink, Eric jumped down from the wall into the lane, off to spend the night who knew where, in one of those safe and secret places all cats have – and a good job too.

CHAPTER 19

The next day, George didn't wake up early as usual.

He didn't go in to sing his good morning hello to The Lady either, even though he knew The Man was definitely not there.

And he didn't even give himself his usual wash after breakfast either – because he didn't eat any breakfast. For George, this was not only highly unusual, but a first.

Instead, he just lay there slumped and curled in a fluffy ginger ball behind the shed, limp and lethargic, his eyes closed to the world and hidden from its horrors with his paws. Only the rising and falling of his fur with his breathing gave any indication that he was still alive.

Dog was worried – he had never seen the old tom like this before. He seemed ill, the way he was hiding from the world, not wanting to see anyone or do anything. The kitten tried to wake him up several times by licking his face and ears, but George just pushed him away. It was all very worrying.

The Lady had left the house ages ago and put food out for George – and, as Dog could see when he went into the kitchen, for him too, in his own saucer. But, when the kitten mentioned breakfast to the old tom, he just miaowed that he wasn't hungry – and didn't even open his eyes at the news of food.

'But you, kitten-cat, must eat – and that's an order!' said George, though his voice was much thinner and quieter than usual.

Reluctantly, Dog obeyed. He had a good feed, followed by a good wash.

And then, as there was no-one at home – (The Lady had been there alone the night before anyway, without The Man, and she had gone out as usual that morning) – it seemed harmless to explore. Dog had only ever been into the kitchen, and he was curious to see what other territory George controlled.

Slowly, and on his guard – despite the apparent absence of any two-legs – Dog padded his way out of the kitchen and into the living room. It all smelt new and strange, and Dog took the opportunity to sniff everything he could. There were the scents of George and The Lady everywhere, especially on the sofa, as would be expected – and the unpleasant stale smoky smell of The Man hung in the air. But there were so many other pongs that Dog's brain was having trouble processing all the information at once.

With some difficulty, he managed to drag himself away from his sniffing of the furniture in the living room, and to go out into the hall, where he stood at the foot of the stairs, gazing up.

Dog had never ever been upstairs in a house before. He'd been on roofs and window ledges, yes, and had peered through windows. But to actually go into the two-legs' sleep-rooms, not to mention their smell-room, was a daring act indeed, and certainly not allowed in the code of cats. The only feline permitted to enter such places was the one whose territory it was, which in this case was George – and some two-legs did not allow even that. But, as there was no-one around, who would know?

The kitten twitched his ears, listening very carefully for any sound that might suggest a two-legs was home or that another cat had followed him into the house. Nothing.

Slowly, gingerly, with his heart beating fast and loud in his little chest, Dog started to climb the stairs.

He came to the smell-room first. He had been in just one of these before, on the ground floor of his old house, but this one looked whiter and brighter. Oddly, it smelt of flowers even though there were none there.

Dog recognised the big white drinking bowl, which is where two-legs sit to make a smell and spray. He had never deigned to drink from one himself, though some animals apparently indulged, which was an uncouth habit, according to George.

He then saw the place where the two-legs wallowed around in their own dirty water, (which was disgusting) or stood in a spray like sky water (which was almost as bad).

Dog gave a little shudder that made his ears itch and tickle. He hurried out of the smell-room and into another which he could tell, from the scent, was The Lady's sleep-room.

The room was beautiful, all soft and fluffy and comfy. It would be the perfect place for a kitten-cat to bed down for a nap – and it was only his growing sense of guilt and anxiety that stopped Dog from doing just that.

He knew he shouldn't be in there – yet he just couldn't help having a look at all the interesting things around him.

The main object in the room was the two-legs' sleep-place – which was big and wide and bouncy, as Dog discovered when he leapt up onto it.

On one side of this was a small table on which stood a lamp, a cup, and a thing with squiggles on it which ticked and tocked. It seemed very silly to Dog that two-legs kept such noisy things by their bedside, and so he wasn't at all surprised that insomnia was a problem for this highly illogical species. There was also another object which was all white in colour and had a twirly wire, like a mouse tail with no end.

On the other side was another table. Various objects were on it, some of which smelt just like The Man. Dog gave a low growl when he sniffed them, but his eye was caught by something on the floor next to the table. It was the bag that Dog had remembered seeing The Man carry into the house the previous day. And, what's more, he could see that its clasp was open.

Dog jumped down and carefully poked his nose into the briefcase. Easing it open, he looked inside. He didn't know what he expected to find, but the bag seemed sort of important-looking and he felt sure that whatever was inside would be interesting in some way.

As it turned out, there were some sealed envelopes which, when Dog bit them gently and lifted them up, seemed awfully heavy and hard, and which also rattled and jingle-jangled when he dropped them back into the bag. This was either very noisy paper, or else he felt sure that there were shiny things in the envelopes – the ones The Man had stolen.

There was also another sealed envelope, which was flat and light, so seemed just to contain paper. Something about it seemed to say that it was the most important of the lot.

Dog considered opening this – he sharpened his teeth and claws every day in anticipation of just such occasions.

But then he realised that there was no point: he wouldn't be able to understand what was written on the paper inside – (he was a cat, after all!)

Moreover, if he opened it, The Man would know his bag had been tampered with, and what terrible two-legs thing would he do then? Added to which, George would be extremely cross. Dog was not even supposed to be in the house, let alone upstairs in The Lady's sleep-room.

Guilt mingled with excitement swirled in Dog's thoughts – something that made his heart skip, his nose tingle and his ears twitch in a peculiarly pleasant manner all at the same time.

Dog sat for a moment wondering what to do. Then, suddenly, the air was filled by the most awful noise. It was coming from the twisty white mouse tail on the bedside table:

'Ringgggg-ringgggg,' it said, 'Ringgggg-ringgggg!'

The thing was alive!

It was the only explanation.

With the lightning speed of a veritable super-cat, Dog jumped off the bed, skidded round the corner, dashed down the stairs, leapt through the living room, careered through the kitchen, and, using his head as a battering ram, clattered through the cat flap at a speed not generally considered conducive to feline health and wellbeing.

He came to a halt behind the shed, panting and yapping in relief at his escape from whatever monster mouse type thing had made that awful sound.

George opened an eye and looked up at the kitten-cat suspiciously.

Dog did what he had been taught to do in such circumstances – he assumed the sitting position, turned his head slightly, and with a look of extreme concentration on his face gave his shoulder a few little innocent licks.

In one slow aching motion, his stiff limbs creaking with the considerable effort, George got to his paws.

'I can see, kitten-cat, that another lesson is called for.'

On the wall, Eric watched George lead Dog out into the garden. He could still see the superstrong catnip between the bins and thought that he might partake of a little later that day. As a long-time stray, he was an experienced recreational user, after all, not some little kitten who didn't know when to stop – though even he would have admitted that stopping took more than a little self-control, something which Eric, by his own admission, most definitely lacked.

'Right,' said George, 'Today the lesson will be all about two-legs.'

Eric was glad to see the old tom up and about. He had seen before how devastating the betrayal of two-legs could be for cats, and knew how sad and angry George would be about The Lady, The Man, everything.

'Two-legs,' started George, clearing his throat with a terse cough and a very deep breath indeed, 'are without doubt the most idiotic, vain, stubborn, selfish, disrespectful, crude, loud, rude, ill-behaved, egotistical, cowardly, inconsistent, inconsiderate, devious, sly, disloyal, greedy, hypocritical, irresponsible, intolerant, unreliable, thoughtless, treacherous, slovenly, filthy, dirty, deranged and stupid creatures on the face of the Earth!'

George ran out of puff at this point and so sucked in another much-needed breath.

Dog gasped a little hiccup of shock; Eric did too, even though he hadn't got a clue what most of those words meant – (but they *sounded* bad, anyway).

'Oh yes,' continued George, the tips of his ears quivering with rage, 'They seem loyal, what with the way they feed you and stroke you and make you purr, but they aren't at all. Betrayal is their game! It's all a deception, a most cunning and deceitful con.'

'George, you feelin' alright?' asked Eric – but the old tom ignored him.

'Two-legs tell us lies – all the time. They say one thing but mean the other. And they are always making promises that they break – as all cats taken to 'the place of smells and pain' well know. In short, they are not to be trusted – ever – and any cat who does so, myself included, is nothing more than a buffoon, an idiot, a nincompoop and a feline fool of the first order.'

'But… George,' said Dog, 'You can't mean that.'

'Oh indeed I do, kitten-cat,' said George, 'The list of the devious and disgusting ways of two-legs is far too long to be taught on this or any other course, or indeed in just one or two lessons. You would need to spend years, kitten, and quite possibly several long lifetimes, in order to fully understand just how horrendous and dangerous two-legs really are.'

'Oh come on, George, they ain't so bad – one or two of 'em, anyways. You's just a bit out o' sorts today, tha'sall!'

'I'll have you know, Eric, that I have never felt better,' said George, a hard dark look solidifying like molten glass in his eyes, 'and I have never seen the world around me with more clarity either. To me, one thing now appears certain. Two-legs are not the friends of cats.

They never have been and never will be. They merely use us as their playthings and their comforters, mere toys to be brought out like dolls and used, and indeed abused. The way they force their attentions on us is nothing less than inter-species harassment!'

'Cor Blimey! Steady on, George, mate,' said Eric, 'The kitten-cat's all ears here.'

'Good! Excellent! Splendid! Then I hope he's listening to every word I say and that he remembers this day forever. You, Eric, are right. No cat needs a two-legs – it is they who need us! They think they can treat us in any way they wish and that we'll just keep on coming back and loving them because we have no choice. Well, we do have a choice – a choice to live free and without two-legs. You seem happy enough as a shameless stray, Eric, so why shouldn't every cat follow your lead?'

Dog turned to Eric, a look of deep concern on his face, his whiskers downturned and drooping in sorrow, his tongue poking out in the manner of a puppy perplexed. It was awful to see George in so much pain, to see him speak so hatefully of two-legs, when he had held them in such high regard before (despite their many disgusting little quirks).

'But George,' said Eric, 'You're *George*, George – the guv'nor – a sophisticated and *heducated* feline what is *impairing* his wisdom and *cleverishness* to the kitten-cat what is 'ere today. I, on the uvver paw, ain't *heducated* like what you is. I ain't no house cat an' never 'ave been, coz I's never 'ad the chance. I'm a stray, George, an' that suits me, coz I ain't ever known nuffink different, not really. But it ain't the fing for most kittens and cats, as you well knows…'

'Ah but maybe it is? Maybe we've just been

deceiving ourselves all this time thinking that we have to be there for two-legs. But why the whiskers should we?!'

'Because… we're cats,' said Eric, 'an' that's what we do, most of us anyways. That's our purpose.'

'Purpose?' yelled George, 'Our *purpose?!*'

His bright yellow eyes were glowing red around the edges, making him look almost as deranged as a doolally dog.

'We have no purpose, other than to eat and sleep and wash, to live and then to die. We should do *just* what we want, as independent cats, as is our right according to the laws of Nature!'

Eric didn't know what to say, so just shook his head at the kitten-cat and gave a supportive wink with his good eye.

'He's not his-self today – he don't mean it,' Eric whispered to Dog.

But George heard it too.

'Oh yes I do. From now on, I too shall be a stray. I too shall come and go as I please, living a life free from duty and honour and responsibility. I too shall delve into dustbins and prowl the alleys in search of nourishment, shunning all company other than that demanded by the most primitive of urges. I too shall step back a million years and watch the world through night-lit eyes unblurred by the illusive affections of false friends from an inferior species. If I want to sleep, I shall sleep. If I want to caterwaul, I shall do so, at any hour of the night. And if I want to lose myself in a fog of catnip, like the most roguish of cats, then I shall do that too. In fact, I feel like losing myself in it right now at this very moment. The lesson has ended, kitten-cat, as has your course. Be a good cat. Goodbye.'

And with that George headed for the catnip pots by the bins.

'*Nooooo!*' miaowed Eric, blocking his way.

'Out of my way, stray!' demanded George, 'Or I shall be forced to use claws.'

'George please,' said Eric, 'this ain't like you at all. You're miaowin' up the wrong tree! Have a sleep, nab a snack, think it over – consider your household, your family, the kitten-cat's education – The Lady… '

'Ha!' said George, indignant, 'The Lady? Huh! She's no lady! She's as common and vulgar as they come, just another tawdry trashy two-legs with the dubious and lewd morals of some mangy worm-ridden alley-cat miaow-around stray!'

'But George – she *loves* you!' pleaded Eric, face to face with his old ginger friend, struggling to stop him from reaching the super-strength catnip and certain, possibly permanent, oblivion.

Eric repeated the words in slow and certain miaows, tom to tom, nose to nose, whisker to whisker:

'The Lady *loves* you, George!'

'*Love?* Ha!'

George almost spat the miaows out.

'There's no such thing as *love!* It's all just self-interest, selfishness, deception and lies – something two-legs have invented to weaken and thus exploit our noble and superior species – not to mention other members of their own. Now out of my way, stray!'

'But George!'

'Go to The Lady, Eric – see if I care – she seems to let anyone into her sleep-room these days, so it might as well be a filthy fleabag layabout like you!'

'Enough!' barked Dog, 'Rrrrf-rrrrf-rrrrf!'

George and Eric froze in shoulder-to-shoulder loggerhead position. They turned round to look at the kitten-cat, whose teeth were now bared scarily as he leant forward, growling like a rabid dog.

'I trusted you, George,' miaowed the kitten-cat, a ghostly reflection of the old tom glistening in the moistness of his eyes, 'And I wanted to learn everything from you about how to be a proper cat, because I know that you are the most successful and marvellous and wonderful feline there is, and the best teacher ever, and I know how much you love The Lady and how much she loves you and... and... I wanted to be just like you George... just like you... '

The kitten-cat's voice broke at the sorrow of these words, and his head hung down as sadly as the old tom's tail.

George said nothing. He just looked at the kitten-cat, thinking.

After a silent moment, Eric spoke:

'Think of the kitten-cat, George, please... '

'Please, George,' echoed Dog, and he miaowed the most plaintive miaow his teacher had ever heard, *'Pleeease... '*

George didn't know what to say. He stared solemnly at the kitten-cat, feeling betrayed and alone, the anger within him melting into the bitterest sadness he had ever felt.

'We're all counting on you, guv'nor,' said Eric, 'Please. The kitten-cat needs you. The Lady needs you. We *all* need you.'

Just then, François appeared on the wall.

'Georges! Georges! Sacrebleu! Zut alors! To come quickly please!'

'For goodness sake, François, can't you see we're busy!' said George, 'And please at least try to use the local Cat dialect, instead of all that foreign claptrap… '

'But Georges,' said François, gravely, 'It eez Mademoiselle Fifi!'

CHAPTER 20

Fifi was in her garden, in a quiet, dark place.

The front of her body was hidden under a shrub, while the back half stuck out, slumped on the lawn. Her tail lay limp by her side in a manner no healthy cat would ever countenance, and her little black button nose was feverishly dry. Fifi was a very sick and ill she-cat indeed.

'I sink she eez seek,' said François, 'she eez look very eel.'

When George and Eric poked their heads into the shrub to talk to her, they could see that she was barely semi-unconscious, though she did respond to her name with a tiny fragile yowl – so different from her usual cheery chirrup-purr.

But her ears did not register the slightest twitch at the miaow-sound of her name – this, in a cat, shows that something is seriously awry.

The toms looked at each other with expressions grave and grim. It was bad – and they knew it.

'I sink zat perhaps Mademoiselle Fifi, she has zer need for zer water,' said François.

'There's gotta be some in her two-legs' kitchen,' said Eric.

'But how on earth can we take Miss Fifi inside, in her state? She is clearly incapable of walking.'

'Nah, guv'nor! We can do it the uvver way – bring the water out to her!'

'Splendid! An excellent idea,' said George, recognising the potential of Eric's suggestion, 'but... '

'I knows what you's gonna say – 'ow does we get the bowl of water to Fifi out 'ere, from inside her 'ouse over there?'

'Precisely!'

George waited for an explanation – but explanation came there none.

'So, how *do* we get the bowl – in the house over there – to Miss Fifi – out here?'

'I ain't got a clue,' said Eric, only now seeing the terrible flaw in his plan.

'Typical stray!' tutted the old tom, 'Never thinks things through... '

'Yeah well, at least I 'ad an idea, 'stead of just moanin'... '

'I was *not* moaning – I was merely being realistic!'

'Don't look like sky water no time soon neither,' said Eric, gazing up at a near-cloudless sky.

'Oh so who's moaning now?' said George.

'Shame really – can't beat the taste. Sort of... *'sky-ey'*... innit?'

'Will you stop thinking about your stomach for once in your life?'

'I know what to do,' miaowed Dog, interrupting.

'Go on,' said George.

Eric winked approval.

'It's just... we don't have to actually carry the bowl out here, do we?'

George, Eric and François looked at each other, then shook their heads in synchronised bafflement.

'Errr… don't we?' said Eric, mid-shake.

'No, we don't,' said Dog, 'We can use ourselves.'

The three cats were still a picture of perfect puzzlement.

'Don't you see?' said Dog, looking from each quizzical whiskery face to the next, 'We can lick up some water from the bowl, hold it inside remembering not to swallow, and then come back outside and dribble it into Miss Fifi's mouth.'

The air was almost filled by the sound of cognitive cogs turning and grinding slowly in the brains of three curious cats.

George pricked up his ears and smiled – as much as any cat can smile, that is.

'A splendid idea!' he said, 'You *see*, the kitten *can* think. I taught him everything he knows, of course. Well done, kitten-cat.'

Dog's chest puffed up with pride at the praise.

'Nice one, kitten,' said Eric – and François smiled at Dog too: he was always particularly fond of inventive and intelligent *chatons*.

So, one by one, the cats went into Fifi's house, licked up a mouthful of water, and returned in line to the place under the shrub where she was sheltering from the world. Then, in turn, they each dripped as much of the mouthful of water as they could onto Fifi's lips – all except Eric, who found that keeping water in his mouth for long periods of time was easier said than done.

The first time he tried, he giggled and the water spilled out. And the second time, he didn't take a deep enough breath so had to spit the water out to avoid choking.

Still, what with George, François and Dog managing to keep up the water convoy, Fifi was at least getting *some* water into her system – essential to avoid dehydration – though she did splutter and cough at times.

They went to get mouthfuls of water for a third time – and were just about to enter the kitchen through the cat flap – when a dark shadow appeared in the kitchen window. The cats ran away from the house and took refuge under a large bush at the end of the garden.

'Fifi!' called a two-legs who came out through the back door, 'Fifi cat! Fifi!'

Dog was about to miaow something when Eric shook his head – a cat must never give away his position in such circumstances, except to two-legs he knows very well indeed, and then only with great caution.

Eventually, the two-legs saw where Fifi's tail was poking out from under a shrub and hurried over to her. Then two small two-legs – (Dog assumed these were kitten two-legs) – came out into the garden. They picked up Fifi and took her inside.

No cat said a thing. George's head was hanging low, and his eyes were damp, no doubt due to all the water he'd spilled earlier while giving a drink to Fifi.

'The place of smells and pain,' whispered Eric to Dog, shaking his head ominously.

François sighed and then turned away, slinking off through the garden to be by himself. There was nothing any of them could do for the she-cat now.

They had all seen fellow felines taken away before, and they usually didn't return, not when they looked as unwell as poor Miss Fifi.

It was time to go home.

George sloped off, his head and tail hanging down defeated as he made his way back forlornly to the wall.

Dog was about to run after him, when he felt Eric's paw on his shoulder.

'Let 'im go, kitten-cat,' he said, 'he needs... to walk alone for a while... '

Dog did what he was told, and he and Eric followed George at a discreet distance, onto the wall and then down into the lane, where their paws began to plod their way back towards George's house. They were all thinking of Fifi – George, especially.

'Fifi was... sort of... y'see... well... George liked Fifi very much,' said Eric, 'and now she's *gawn*... '

'*Gawn?*' queried the kitten-cat.

'The very same,' miaowed Eric, '*Gawn* away forever, like what we all does one day, when our nine lives is up. I'll have a proper whiskers-to-whiskers with the old tom later – ow's that sound?'

Dog nodded. There was nothing he wanted to say, with either a miaow or a yap – he just couldn't find the words somehow.

'George just needs... time... kitten... '

Though, as George turned the corner of the lane he realised that he might not have very much time left to mourn Miss Fifi after all – for there, facing him, were three enormous black dogs.

They were lying down sleeping in the lane and, for the briefest of moments, George thought that maybe he hadn't disturbed them, that maybe he could just back away and go the long way round to get back home.

No such luck. The biggest of the dogs had one of its

horrible eyes open, as black and shiny as a slug, and it was looking straight at him!

A shiver cold as winter sky water trickled down George's spine.

In a flash, he turned on his heels and ran back to where Eric and Dog were trailing behind.

'Run!' he miaowed as he approached, 'Run away! Now!'

The loud barking that immediately followed this suggestion meant that neither had to ask why.

The three cats ran as fast as they could up the lane – which was uphill now.

Dog looked back. The three black dogs behind them were huge, especially the one in the middle, with very sharp-looking white teeth. And they never stopped barking and growling and snarling:

'Rrrrrrrr!' they said, 'Rrrroffff-rrrroffff-rrrrofffff!'

But then, dogs did have such a noticeably limited vocabulary! And their slobbering and dribbling of saliva everywhere was a disgusting doggy habit that George would no doubt have commented on severely had he not been otherwise engaged in running for his life.

Eric ran fast up the hill, the kitten close behind. All they needed to do was outrun the beasts, or at least match their speed, until they found a wall low enough to jump onto – and from there go into a garden, or some other hidey-hole, where no dog could ever stick its snout.

'Up here!' yelled Eric, heading for a wall.

But Dog was not looking in Eric's direction. Instead, he was leaning over his shoulder to look back at the dogs.

Because George – a mature and well-fed cat who was not as nimble on his paws as he used to be – was in trouble. The three black dogs were definitely gaining on him as he panted and puffed his way up the hill.

'Eric!' yowled Dog.

Eric looked back from the wall where he was now out of danger. He could see that George wasn't going to make it.

But what could he do?

There was no way that he or the kitten-cat would survive an encounter with hounds like these. He'd been in enough scrapes himself to know that this would be a close call too many.

'You gotta save yerself!' Eric called to Dog.

'But what about… ?'

'Run!' ordered George, 'Leave me here, kitten, and run! I'll be alright.'

The dogs were so close to the old tom now – they'd be on him in seconds.

'C'mon, kitten-cat!' shouted Eric, 'Up here, quick!'

'Save yourself, kitten-cat!' yelled George, 'And that's an order!'

But Dog didn't obey George or jump up to Eric on the wall. Instead, he skidded to a halt on the lane in a cloud of dust, turned around on his heels and started running back towards the three terrifying black dogs that were nearly upon the old ginger tom.

Eric couldn't believe what he was seeing. Already that day, they'd lost Fifi, and it was now only a matter of time before George went the same way – (and to lose two fellow felines in one day would certainly be a tragedy, not to mention a little bit careless).

And now the kitten-cat in his foolishness was

heading back straight into the jaws of doggy death and doom, when he could have escaped!

There was a fine line between courage and stupidity, and Eric thought that the kitten-cat may well have just bounded across it in the latter direction.

But the stray had to go and help him. How could he not? Even if it was suicidal...

Eric took a deep breath – a final sniff of the air he was sure he would soon no longer be breathing – then jumped off the wall and dashed down the lane.

Meanwhile, George was now galumphing up the lane towards Dog, the hounds hot on his heels.

'You silly kitten-cat!' he panted, 'I told you to run!'

But then, instead of Dog stopping when he reached George, he ran straight past him towards the three black dogs in pursuit.

Eric could hardly bear to look. The kitten-cat was just a little ball of black-and-white fluff compared to these huge dog-monsters. He wouldn't even make much of a meal for them either – just a saliva-stimulating starter snack before the main course.

And then the stray realised that he and George would be the main course, so tried to stop thinking of anything. That was the problem with thinking – it always made you worried and unhappy. Far better to be like him and not think much at all on your journey through life – it was far safer and happier that way, all things considered.

The kitten-cat hurtled down the lane, heading straight for the largest of the beasts – the one in the middle – the top dog. He was big and black and terrible, with nasty wolf-like eyes, and huge teeth gnashing and snarling in his powerful jaws.

Even a two-legs would struggle to fight one dog like that, let alone three, and now Dog was trying to do it all on his own!

Oh the foolishness of youth!

Eric squinted his one good eye as he watched the kitten-cat's suicide mission in horror. With a resigned sigh, he followed in his wake, as did George, who had by now turned round (which took a while, at his age) and was following after Eric straight towards the terrifying trio of dogs.

Then, something happened – something strange and magical and wonderful.

Instead of fighting – instead of being torn paw from little black-and-white paw by those big slobbering doggy teeth – the kitten-cat just stopped, and then started barking and yapping, in exactly the way George had been teaching him *not* to do.

'Rrrrufff-rruffff-rrufff-rfrfrfrf-rffff-yap-yap-yapppp-rrrrufffff-ffff-ffff!!!'

When the dogs heard this, the look of crazed fury left their snarling faces. They skidded to a halt, a cloud of dust mushrooming around them.

The expression now on their faces was one of complete and utter bafflement and confusion – (even more so than usual for dogs).

For there, right in front of them, was a cat – (not a dog, but a cat) – and a young cat at that, more of a kitten – (and a kitten, not a puppy) – but this animal was not, as would be expected, speaking Cat.

No – *he was speaking Dog!!!*

(And speaking it rather well too, it had to be admitted.)

The two subservient dogs on either side looked at

their leader, who was listening intently to what the kitten-cat was barking in his direction.

Eric lifted up his paw and scratched his ear – hard, with one of his tough sharp claws – just to make sure he wasn't dreaming. He wasn't, but he should've been. For there before him was a little black-and-white kitten-cat yapping and growling at three huge black dogs who were now sitting obediently before him, heads bowed, ears limp, tails still, as if being reprimanded by their master.

Slowly, with their tails between their legs and heads bowed in submission, they sloped off and left Dog standing there in the middle of the lane.

The kitten turned round to where George and Eric stood, open-jawed and stunned into miaow-less silence.

'It's safe now,' he said with a satisfied flick of his white-tipped tail – a tail which Eric was now convinced was probably an actual real magician's wand. A magic spell was all that could explain the amazing spectacle that they had all just witnessed.

George and Eric blinked at each other, but said nothing – which is, according to cat etiquette, the only advisable response in the most unfamiliar and baffling situations.

So instead, they just followed Dog up onto the wall.

It was time to go home.

CHAPTER 21

'There won't be any more problems,' said Dog, 'I think I made everything clear to them – as clear as sky water actually.'

George and Eric nodded, though nothing was as clear as sky water to them. As clear as muddy puddles maybe...

'The big angry one in the middle was in charge, so I only had to talk to him to control the others. And I told him that if he ever chased cats again, then we'd let all dogs everywhere know about how they ran away terrified from a little kitten-cat. Do you think I was too harsh?'

Eric and George shook their heads in unison, jaws still hanging open, overcome by amazement at the miracle they had just seen. By happy coincidence, their faces bore an expression uncannily similar to the stunned look that was frozen onto the dogs' faces when the kitten-cat confronted them.

'You have to be noisy and strict with dogs, or they just won't listen. They can be... *funny*... like that... '

'Oh yeah,' muttered Eric, '*Habsolutely* 'ilarious... '

'But kitten-cat, how? I mean... when? I mean... how?'

It was no good: George was completely at a loss. Eric took over:

'What the old tom is wonderin', like, is *hexactly* 'ow you did what you done – what wiv all the dog lingo malarkey an' that, innit? See?'

'Mais oui, d'accord,' said François, who had just appeared on the wall, 'I was watch what 'as 'appened, an' 'ow ziss petit chat 'as, 'ow you say, put zem in zer house of zer dogs!'

'The *dog house*,' said George, wearily, '*Put them in the dog house* – that's the phrase. Can't anyone round here speak standard Cat any more?'

'You all knew I spoke Dog,' continued the kitten, 'and did doggy things like wagging my tail and yapping – that's why you're giving me lessons, George, to teach me how to be a proper cat. Isn't it?'

'Ah yes, kitten-cat,' said George, 'We naturally heard you yapping and barking and woofing, making the most dreadful and unnatural noises a cat can ever make – and many more times than we would have liked – but I... we... didn't actually think that all that noisy doggy nonsense actually *meant* anything.'

'I did,' said Eric.

'Eric, no you did not – don't lie,' said George, cross at the stray's continual mis-miaowing, 'And will you please stop doing that!'

Eric had several blades of grass sticking out from his mouth and was busy chewing the juice out of them.

'Pardon me, guv'nor,' said the stray, spitting out the stalks.

George tutted.

'Chewing grass is a private activity and should be undertaken only when necessary and well out of the sight of both two-legs and vulnerable kitten-cats.'

'S'just… I felt like nibblin' some grass – so I did. Same fing always 'appens when I gets a bit nervous. I's in shock – like what we all is… '

'We can't all just do what we feel like doing, Eric. If we did that then we'd be no better than a common puppy chasing his own tail, and might as well be living in a world run by dogs.'

'Well, I likes chasing my own tail,' grumbled Eric.

George closed his eyes in weary resignation. He was grateful when François took over his line of questioning:

'*Alors*… so… 'ow you are learn ziss strange and mysterieux language of zer dogs, mon petit?'

'Exactly,' said George, 'ow… I mean, *how*… on earth did you learn it? Where? When? And, not to put too fine a point on it, *why?*'

'Yeah, c'mon, tell us – we's gotta know! Let the cat out 'o the bag, kitten! 'Ow comes you can speak the Dog lingo, like?'

The cats sat in a circle around Dog, eager for him to tell his tale, obedient pupils waiting for their lesson to begin.

'Well,' Dog said, 'it all started when I was a kitten… '

'You still is a kitten,' said Eric.

'Shhh!' snapped George, 'Let the cat speak!'

'I used to live – before I came here and met George on the wall – in a big old house, which must have been a long way away because it took me many moons travelling before I reached here.'

George's ears twitched, and he gave his paw a little lick. He really did not like to be reminded of the day he met Dog, and all that nasty business with the wall.

'I suppose I must have been birthed there, but I never knew my mother, or my father.'

'Not unusual,' sighed George, 'more's the pity… '

And he gave a good long stare at Eric who was rumoured to have sired several litters of kittens with shameless she-cats in the vicinity.

'Anyway, in this big old house, there lived an old lady two-legs. And she had lots and lots of cats – more than I could count at that young kitten age.'

'Sounds like an intelligent two-legs,' said George, approvingly.

'Yes,' said Dog, 'but she also had lots and lots of dogs.'

'Why is it,' pondered George, 'that two-legs are always their own worst enemies?'

'But,' said Dog, 'we didn't fight – not much anyway – and we all got on well together. If there was ever a skirmish then the lady two-legs would be very cross, and get very upset, and none of us wanted to see that, so we all stuck to our own places and had our own food and water. And… well… that's all I can remember. I didn't have any mum-cat, like the other kittens there, so I spent all my time with the puppies and dogs, and I sort of picked up the language and the, y'know, tail-wagging and tongue-poking and yapping – that sort of thing. And that's why everyone called me Dog!"

'Zen what 'as 'appened?' said François, leaning forward on his paws.

'One day, I was out in the garden with the old lady two-legs – she was out putting big white wings on the line – they were from her sleep-room, I think. I miaowed *hello* at her and she bent down to pat me and stroke me like she always did, and then she looked sort of sad and in pain, and then… '

Dog closed his eyes at the memory. He hadn't

thought of the old lady two-legs and the big old house for a long time, because it made him so unhappy.

'I went and put a paw on the old lady two-legs' face, but she didn't move and she went so cold too – colder even than a happy cat's nose. Later on, they came and took her away in a big white wheel-box. For a while we thought she would be coming back, but gradually some of the cats started to leave – we had no food there, so needed to hunt, to move on into new territories looking for prey.'

'See – you don't need no two-legs if you's a nifty mouser…'

'Shhh Eric please,' said George, 'Continue, kitten-cat.'

'Then, one day, they came – lots and lots of two-legs – and took the dogs away.'

'Hoorah! Bring out the biscuits!' said Eric, paws in the air.

'Oh no,' said Dog, 'they were my friends, you see. One of them told me to run and hide when he saw the two-legs coming, so I hid at the end of the garden, behind a thorny bush where I couldn't be seen, but where I could see everything and everyone.'

'Well-chosen, kitten-cat – sounds a splendid place for cats.'

'Purrr-fect!' miaowed Eric, rolling over with a wink.

'One of the dogs gave me a little whimper which means *"Stay there!"* in Dog. So I did. And soon, the two-legs took all the dogs away and I was left all alone in the garden of that big old house.'

'So you had no two-legs to feed you, no warm house to sleep in, no-one at all?' said George.

Dog nodded. He remembered how very alone he had felt back then.

172

'For a while, I stayed put, wondering what to do, hoping the old lady two-legs – and the cats and the dogs – would come back. But no-one came back. Not for ages. Not at all. So that's when I decided I had to leave that place – had to walk away and find somewhere else to live. And then, after a few adventures, I found all of you – George, Eric, François – my friends.'

It was a very sad story, and Dog felt very sad in the telling of it.

'Oh c'est dommage,' sighed François, and he remembered his lost loves with an overwhelming melancholy that dampened his beautiful eyes to the colour of the darkest green glass, 'Ziss eez so sad… '

Eric and George nodded morosely.

All cats knew loneliness, but, unlike two-legs, were self-sufficient and self-contained enough to bear it. That, however, did not mean they didn't want to make the acquaintance of any other cats, or indeed two-legs – in fact, quite the reverse.

'Cor Blimey – what a start in life!'

'Sacrebleu!' sighed François, 'Zut alors! Quel dommage!'

'Funny 'ow we's never *arksed* you 'bout any o' that before, eh, kitten cat?' miaowed Eric.

'Indeed it is,' said George, making a mental note to be more inquisitive and curious about incomers in future.

'Just sink, Georges,' said François, 'zat eef ziss kitten-cat have not learn to speak in zer language of zer dogs – zen you and 'im would not be 'ere, non?'

'Y'ain't wrong there, mate,' said Eric, 'We'd all've be *dead-ified* good an' proper if the kitten wouldn't't've saved the day… '

Just then, a bird high up in the neighbour's tree began tweeting a tweet just like the ones George remembered from his youth. Soon, the memories came flooding back.

He thought back to his teacher, the old black tom, who had taught him so much, cared for him so conscientiously, and done his duty as a noble and honourable cat by helping a kitten in need.

He thought of just how much he owed that old tom. And he thought of his duty, and what he had to do.

And – after all that had happened, all the trials and set-backs, and all the terrible pain – he finally remembered what it was to be George again. And he knew his duty remained undone.

The old tom bowed his head in shame and closed his eyes tight shut. He thought of how selfish he had been, how inconsiderate of Dog's feelings – of how his humiliation at the hands of The Man, and the overwhelming sadness at the loss of Miss Fifi, had turned him – George, a noble and well-mannered cat – into a brute, a conceited and arrogant fool, as ill-mannered as the worst stray and ruffian on the street, and – though it pained him to say it – as stupid and simple-minded as a dog, (which, for a cat, is a terrible fate indeed).

'By my paws,' sighed George, getting to his feet, 'François, you are right – and Eric too. If it were not for the kitten-cat here, and his ability to speak Dog – not forgetting his fearless and selfless bravery – then I, for one, would no longer be here miaowing and yowling in my garden today.'

George turned to Dog, and bowed as low as his tail.

'Thank you, kitten-cat, for saving my life – or one of

my lives, at least – and we all know how short they can be,' said George, and they all thought of poor little Fifi and other absent friends, 'I have been a very silly and selfish cat indeed. I am truly sorry for my behaviour. Please forgive me, kitten.'

Dog said nothing. He just smiled and wagged his tail in delight. Happily, he managed to suppress a very definite yap that, in his pre-education days, would have just been blurted out, so he was definitely getting better at being a cat, for sure – thanks to his teacher.

He reached out and put a paw on George's shoulder, then touched noses with him – which, as all felines (and some of the more observant two-legs) know is Cat for '*I forgive you*'.

Eric perked his ears up at this. He thought George would never snap out of the awful gloom that had engulfed him, so was delighted to see the old tom back to normal.

François had seen it all before, that dread darkness that can drive two-legs and their cats mad in distant lands, at times when their shame and isolation make their minds fight against them far more viciously than any enemy ever could.

'You,' announced George with pride, 'are a cat.'

'I am a cat!'

'Splendid!' said George

'Splendid!' echoed Dog – and Eric and François joined in too.

'You are a masterpiece of nature, the most marvellous of creatures, the paragon of animals. How noble in aspect, how infinite in wisdom, how delightful in disposition. The most perfect pet imaginable – and the most free and admirable and independent four-legged possessor of fur in the world. Elegant, dignified, poised...'

'Poised,' repeated Dog, Eric and François in unison, proud of every word George miaowed loudly into the evening air.

'You are masterful, noble, intelligent, wise, creative, fascinating, captivating, charming, loving, seductive, engaging, winsome, brave, self-assured, athletic, elegant, handsome, beautiful, well-mannered, lovely, irresistible and sweet.'

'Sweet!' miaowed the cat chorus – and what intelligent and perceptive creature could possibly disagree?

'Naturally, with such gifts come great responsibilities. There are certain standards, certain ways, certain traditions – of dignity, honour, duty and well-deserved pride that must be observed.'

No cat demurred. They all knew the privileged status they enjoyed in life, and how two-legs needed their help. Even a cat without a two-legs like Eric knew how weak they were, what with their awful evolutionary eye and ear disabilities and their weird fur-free skin disorder.

'This is a matter of some urgency because, as we all know, The Lady is in danger, so I am pleased to say,' announced George, 'that I have a new plan.'

The cats huddled close around him to listen. They wondered what idea he had come up with now.

'It is all perfectly simple,' said George, 'We have to make sure that The Lady knows all about The Man – that he's a cad, a rogue, a thief, a liar, a wrong 'un.'

'A wrong 'un!' repeated Eric, Dog and François.

'And we must do that by using not only our brute strength – claws and teeth and that kind of thing – but by using our most marvellous feline minds. Our innate cunning and cleverness. Our brains.'

'Brains!' miaowed the cats.

'It is our duty and our honour to protect The Lady, to keep her from whatever harm The Man intends to inflict upon her, to fight with all our might against those who would want to destroy our superior and civilised way of life, whatever the cost may be. Is that clear?' said George.

'Clear as sky water!' sang the cats, and they huddled round and got down to the business of working out the plan in detail, late into the night.

CHAPTER 22

It was the day of the attack.

The cats sat silent and secret in the garden, deep in anticipatory thought, paws crossed for luck.

They knew in their whiskers that if this didn't work, then the consequences would be grave – both for them and for The Lady – and that the world would never be the same again.

It would be a *cat*astrophe of *cat*aclysmic proportions indeed, and would mean that George would lose his home, his territories, his two-legs – and thus would be unable to teach the kitten how to be a cat, leaving his education half-complete. And who else was there to supervise such an important educational undertaking?

More than that, the pride of an entire species was at stake.

Success was therefore vital. The alternative didn't bear thinking about.

It was, as Eric reminded every cat there present, 'The most *serious-est* situation – ever!' In that garden, anyway.

Eric felt like doing a smell, so did one, which George thought was typical. If a cat wants a chair and a two-legs is in it, then such uncouth behaviour may well occasionally be permitted; but at times like these, it ill behoves a cat to be both indiscreet and inconsiderate to others. Tense and nervous tummy aches of anticipation were perfectly understandable – but there is a time and place…

'Whoops!' said Eric, but only after the others' nostrils had started twitching at the pong, 'Bit nervous 'ere… S'cuse I… '

'And could you please stop *that* too, Eric!' snapped George.

Eric spat out the grass stalks he had been chewing nervously.

'Sorry all,' he sniffed.

Then he resumed his position behind the shed with George and Dog, before giving a cheeky wink to the kitten-cat, which always cheered them both up.

François was not with them. He was on the shed roof, in position.

Then they heard the front door open – for long enough for a two-legs couple to walk through it – and close. That meant that The Lady was home. The booming deep voice that they heard soon after confirmed that The Man was with her.

Eric closed his good eye and tried concentrating on future success to boost his confidence.

George took deep breaths to try and settle his nerves. He was worrying if his considerable plumpity would make him slower on his feet during the approaching battle – and if that would make him a burden and put fellow cats at risk.

François was lying low, flat against the shed roof, having a little meditative siesta.

And Dog thought back to the old lady two-legs who had kept him as a kitten, to all the cats and the dogs he'd known, to all his friends past and present – including George's two-legs, The Lady, who had been so kind to him and who was now in such terrible danger herself.

He knew that this was quite probably the most important day in his life thus far (though he had only seen one summer), but he was sure there would be plenty of other important days in future – *if* they could all survive this one, that is. It was a big *'if'*.

Dog knew in his whiskers that George was right. It was every cat's duty to defend his two-legs, whatever the cost may be.

And though The Lady was not strictly *his* two-legs, she had fed him well (even if The Man had forced her to reduce rations) and she didn't seem to mind if George's friends stayed in the garden either. If only all two-legs could be like her, then no cat would ever be hungry or unwanted or stray, and no two-legs would ever be unlooked-after, unhappy and lonely either, not with so many cats around to care for them.

'Just going out for a smoke,' called The Man, unlocking the back door.

'OK – I'm having a quick shower,' The Lady replied, making George's heart pang heavily: she used to call his name all the time using the same soft and gentle voice.

'Yeeeuuukkk!' said Eric with a shudder, thinking about the deranged two-legs' activity of standing naked in hot and heavy indoor sky water.

'Steady,' whispered George, to himself as well as the other cats.

They watched The Man step into the garden. Dog looked back at George, who put a gentle paw on the kitten-cat's shoulder to reassure him.

The Man lit his cigarette. It was a warm late Spring

evening, with sun-speckled clouds drifting lazily across the sky: the lull before the coming storm.

'Wait for it!' whispered George, hoping that François on the roof would do so.

'Wait for it!'

And then it happened.

'Arrrggghhh!' yelled The Man, 'My eyes, my eyes!'

François stood on the roof of the shed, his back to The Man, squirting a jet of spray into the two-legs' face, right into the eyes.

It was no ordinary wee either. François knew from well-travelled experience which foods and liquids caused certain effects to occur in that bodily excretion, so had rummaged around in restaurant bins the evening before to find the most exotically spicy and hot morsels he could – all the better to give that acidic chilli-heat burning effect to the stream of spray that was now stinging The Man's eyes.

'Now!' ordered George, and the cats ran from behind the shed towards The Man, who was by now staggering with one hand (in which he still held his 'smoke-stick') out-stretched and feeling for obstacles, while the other rubbed his reddening eyes.

George, Eric and Dog jumped onto The Man's legs simultaneously, scratching and biting into his trousered flesh, from the ankles upwards. To unbalance The Man – knock him off his feet – was key, George knew, and this was the strategy.

Eric then scrambled right up The Man's back and started scramming his scalp.

Meanwhile, George clawed at the place between The Man's legs and Dog bit hard into his ankles.

'Arrrggghhh!' screamed The Man, blinking in near-blindness as the pain engulfed him, 'Owwwww-oww-oww!'

The cats spat and scrammed, inflicting considerable hurt on the two-legs, and François, whose bladder was now as empty as a puppy's skull, came down from the shed roof to join in too.

But their adversary was a big Man two-legs, and strong, even if his eyes were half-blind with the most powerfully spicy wee François had ever produced (which left him sorer in his nether regions than he would have liked too).

With one enormous yank, The Man pulled Eric from his back as if peeling off a Velcro fastener, and threw him down with considerable force – though fortunately he landed in the bed of nasturtiums, which broke his fall somewhat.

Then he punched George to the ground, and shook François and Dog from his legs and ankles like falling fruit – so that now all the cats lay around stunned and aching on the garden lawn and path.

'Bloody rabid animals!' screamed The Man, in a high-pitched pain-ridden voice, 'I'll put the lot of you down myself!'

And with that, he gave an almighty kick at the cats.

Fortunately, the kick just missed François, who scrambled up to the shed roof out of reach.

George, however, was too old and slow to move out of the way. He knew and accepted that his plumpity meant he would not get away from The Man's boot.

Just before The Man kicked him, he signalled to Dog:

'Now, kitten-cat! Now! Get the evidence! And that's an order!'

Which The Man heard as:

'Miiiiiaaaaaooooowwwwww-yowwwww-www-yowww-wowwww-miaow-miaow-miaow!'

Reluctant to leave George, but knowing that he had to follow his orders for the attack to work, Dog dashed past The Man and hurtled through the cat flap into the house. So he did not see The Man's boot kick the old tom and send him flying through the air like a football, only to land in a rubbery shrub some distance away.

'Take that you fat useless old ginger fleabag!' he yelled, 'Damn feral animals – I'll exterminate the lot of you, I will!'

Eric and François hissed at The Man, who grinned at the effectiveness of his good hard kick – they (and he) knew he was winning. He then took a long hard drag of his cigarette and puffed out the smoke, smugly certain of victory.

'I'm calling the council – vermin department. They'll dispose of you, alright – prob'ly make you into tennis racket strings or glue!'

With a smirk smeared on his face like blood, he walked towards the house, still rubbing his eyes, but also stroking his scalp where Eric had caused not a little damage by digging deep into the skin with his razor-sharp claws.

But then something strange happened.

The sky grew dark, the birds were silenced, and the air hung heavy with the first low growl of a harbinger of doom – for The Man anyway.

The cats all looked over to the wall. There, crouched low as a groan, was the huge grey form of The Bruiser, his piercing yellow eyes fixed on The Man, his rumbling growl a sign of imminent danger to any animal that hears it (for those who can understand Cat, anyway).

The Man tutted:

'Not another one,' he scoffed, 'You're breeding like flies out here! I'll have the lot of you gassed, I will, and…'

But he did not finish his sentence – because just then The Bruiser launched himself with a giant tiger-like leap right onto his upper back. There, he began to scratch and bite at The Man's neck and scalp, all whilst making the most ear-piercing blood-curdling screeching hiss that the cats had ever heard.

'Arrrrrgggggghhhhh! Help! Help! I'm being attacked by a rabid cat! Arrrrrgggggghhhhh! HELP ME!!!'

The screams were so loud that even The Lady, who was upstairs in the shower, heard them, and so did Dog, who at that very moment had his nose in The Man's briefcase in the sleep-room. He had finally found the envelope he was looking for and emerged with it clenched tightly in his mouth, looking for all the world like a feline postman.

Dog dashed downstairs, skirting past the bathroom door just as The Lady, towel on head and another around her, opened it. All she saw was a black-and-white blur heading for the stairs, but the noise and commotion of what was going on outside soon took over her attention.

She went straight downstairs, in slippers and dressing gown, in the direction of the shouts and screams.

When she reached the kitchen she saw it: a massive grey cat straddling the back of The Man, biting and scratching his head and face and neck raw with its teeth and claws.

There was no sign of George, but she noticed a tabby

on the shed roof and what looked like a scruffy black-and-grey stray in the nasturtium bed she had planted. She could also see, sitting near the back door, the small black-and-white kitten-cat that she remembered from the other day.

'Help!' yelled The Man, 'Heeeeelp!'

The Lady went out of the house and the huge grey cat, as if startled by the presence of another two-legs, unclawed itself from The Man's flesh, dropped down onto the garden path, and with just a few giant bounding leaps was up on the wall at the end of the garden. Then he was gone, off down into the lane to his lair.

The Man stumbled after it, to the wall at the end of the garden, and looked down into the lane, only to come face to face with three huge black dogs barking up at him.

'I hope you rip him paw from paw,' snarled The Man, 'I've always been a dog person anyway...'

The dogs, however, did not move from where they stood, strands of saliva dripping like blood from their growling mouths. And The Man couldn't help getting the distinct feeling that perhaps these dogs were not on his side after all. In fact, he had the awful suspicion that they were actually supporting the cats, which seemed to him as mad as everything else that had happened that day.

When The Lady looked again at the roof of the shed, the tabby cat was gone, as was the scruffy dirty-looking stray in her nasturtiums.

And it had all happened in seconds.

But now at least she could see George, who was limping towards her from the end of the garden.

'They're all vermin!' screamed The Man, 'Rabid,

disgusting, disease-ridden, dangerous scum – that's what these cats are!'

'Are you alright? Shall I call an ambulance?'

'Nah – just scratches. They're just dumb animals after all. Council pest control – the extermination department – that's who we need to cleanse this place of feline filth!'

The Lady was just about to go inside to phone them, when she felt a soft furry paw padding at her ankles. It was the young black-and-white cat from before, who was hum-miaowing as loud as he could, on account of having something stuck in his mouth.

An envelope – definitely an envelope.

The Lady bent down and took it from the kitten-cat's mouth.

'Miiiiiaaaaaooooow-yow-yow-yow!' said George, who, despite his many aches and pains, was overjoyed to see that the kitten-cat had done his duty, and with exceptional courage and honour too.

The Lady opened the envelope and pulled out a document.

'What's this… ?' she muttered to herself.

She unfolded the paper and started reading. As she did so, her expression changed.

The Lady looked at Dog, and then at George, with a face that both cats knew meant 'Sorry' – in two-legs' language, anyway.

'I'll grab the fat old ginger one now,' said The Man, 'and this little black-and-white runt.'

'Oh no you won't!' said The Lady.

The Man was confused. Why did she seem suddenly so angry when moments before she'd been all sympathy?

'We've got to call the council now,' he said, 'Get rid of this vermin scum for good!'

'The only vermin scum around here is you!' said The Lady, her angry eyes glaring accusingly at The Man. The words hit him like a blade in the brain.

'I don't understand… ' said The Man, and then he saw the envelope, 'What's that?'

'You know what it is. It's an inventory – a list of assets – my property – house, jewellery, everything.'

'I… I… can explain… ' stuttered The Man, realising now that The Lady held in her hands the letter he kept sealed in his briefcase (which he was sure he had kept locked).

'It states here in a note – and I quote: *"Marry soon, divorce in three years, take 50% of the assets, retire. Job done."* End of quote.'

The words echoed their treachery on the air.

'I can explain… ' mumbled The Man, rumbled and exposed.

The cats – George, Dog, and also Eric and François who were sitting behind the shed – stared at him: this disgraceful, dishonourable, shameful creature, this lying deceitful thief, this most reprehensible wrong 'un of a two-legs that any of them had ever had the misfortune to wag their tails at.

'There's also an inventory of items – and I quote – *"already acquired"* … '

'They're upstairs,' confessed The Man, 'I… I was just taking them to be valued, for safekeeping, yeah?'

But The Lady was having none of it.

'Get out!' she yelled, in an ear-splittingly shrieking voice that George had never heard her use before, 'Get out now!'

'But I can explain,' said The Man, for a final time.

'Leave now or I'll call the police!'

The Man could tell from The Lady's look that she meant it too. His pleading open face hardened into a pinched expression of exposure and defeat.

He turned around to look at the cats. All eyes were on him like spotlights – or possibly *cats' eyes*, he thought.

It was all over.

With a bitter little tut and a shake of his disbelieving head – but without even meeting The Lady's eyes – he brushed past her back into the house. She checked that he left immediately too, without his briefcase or any of her 'shiny things'.

'And don't come back!' The Lady yelled, slamming the front door behind him.

The cats watched The Man's wheel-box zoom down the street and swing round the corner so fast it almost ran into another wheel-box, which beeped loudly.

George gave his shoulder a lick, before turning to Dog and the other cats.

'By my paws,' he miaowed, 'I do believe that we have won the day!'

They were all exhausted, as well as bruised and hurt – though none seemed seriously damaged – and so the celebration was muted, a sense of relief rather than triumph welling in every pussycat's breast at this great victory.

And then Eric began sniffing the air.

'Can anyone smell burnin'?' he said.

Noses twitched in unison, keen as ever to sample any scent carried on the breeze.

'Mais oui,' sniffed François, 'C'est le feu ici... 'ow you say... I can to smell zerr fire... '

And then Dog saw it:

'Eric, your furry coat – it's on *fire!*' he said.

The stray turned his head back to see – in horror – the long black-and-grey fur on his back ablaze. Just visible, nestling within the inferno was the smouldering end of The Man's discarded 'smoke-stick'.

'The pond – quick!' ordered George.

And with that, Eric ran as fast as he could to the wall, jumped upon it, and then launched himself through the air in a trajectory that he hoped would end with him plummeting into the large round pond in the middle of the next-door neighbours' garden.

Down, down, down he fell.

And then, with an almighty splash, Eric plopped into the middle of the pond.

The fire was immediately extinguished, though this obvious advantage was balanced by the distinct disadvantage of both him and his fur now being completely submerged underwater, which is certainly not the sort of place a feline ever wants to find himself – not without very good reason indeed.

CHAPTER 23

All's *fur* in love and war, as two-legs sometimes say, and none of the cats who witnessed the events that day would have disagreed, all things considered.

They had won a great victory, one that would live forever in the memory of cats – and, most importantly, The Lady was now safe.

It had been a very close call indeed, but now The Man was gone forever.

George could see that The Lady was no longer under his spell, that the brainwashing he had so cruelly used to control her was now expertly excised, and that the enemy was utterly vanquished.

So everything was back as it should be, with George the centre of The Lady's attention, and proud to be devoted at all times to ensuring her comfort and well-being – as well as being focused on the essential continuation of the kitten-cat's education.

It had been the most awful of experiences, and very nearly resulted in serious injury to many an animal. But now, thanks to the cleverness, dignity, bravery and unblemished honour of felines, the world was put to rights, the true balance and order of the universe restored, and all was well with the world and the cats within it.

All except for Eric, that is.

'Ow ow ow!' he miaowed. 'Stop it stop it stop it! It tickles!'

'Stay still, Eric, and stop squealing like a kitten. It's for your own good.'

'Yeah, I knows that, but it ain't stopping all the *tickle-ification* though, innit?'

Eric stood dripping wet in the middle of the garden, with George, François and Dog licking him dry. It was a job that had to be done.

It is a truth generally acknowledged, even by the dimmest of two-legs, that cats and water do not mix – (unless the liquid is taken in via the miaowing end of a feline for the express purpose of relieving thirst) – and thus are best kept as far apart as possible at all times. However, emergency situations sometimes call for emergency solutions – and if that involves jumping into a very watery pond to put out a fire on one's fur, and thereby getting all wet and soggy, so be it.

Fortunately, what with all the cats licking Eric's fur, he was soon much less damp – but no-one expected what happened next.

When the cats stood back to admire the end result of their drying operation, they saw something that made their jaws fall open in shock. For there before them was a cat called Eric who did not look in the least like the stray they had known.

Instead, they found themselves face to face with a huge bouffant puff-ball of a fluffy pompom-shaped cat, with a head at one end, a big bushy tail at the other, and four barely-visible fluffy-pawed feet sticking out underneath.

'What?' said Eric, wondering why the cats were staring at him, 'What is it?'

'But Eric,' gasped Dog in something approaching wonder, 'your fur… It's… '

'It's… black… and… *white*,' said George, genuinely surprised, 'not black and *grey*. Splendid! You see before you, kitten, indisputable evidence of the importance of regular washing. Look what happened when such ablutions were neglected; see how a thorough wash restored not only a cat's cleanliness and dignity, but also the true colour of his coat.'

'Mais, he eez look comme un nuage… 'ow you say?… like a cloud who eez most fluffy!' chuckled François.

'You look just like a pompom!' giggled Dog, tongue a-poke.

Eric frowned. Like all cats, he especially disliked being laughed at – something which, ironically, he could hear much better now that his ears had been cleaned out with pond water.

Looking peeved, he jumped on the wall so that he could see his reflection in the shed window. But when he peered at himself in the glass with his one good eye, he almost wished that he'd lost that too so he wouldn't have to gaze upon the monstrous vision before him.

His ears pricked up and his fur stood on end in horror – which arguably made him look even more like a big round fluffy pompom than he did already.

'Miiiiiaaaaaoooooowwwww-wowww-wowww!' he wailed, 'Cor Blimey, I'm *fluffy-ified! Pompom-ificated* – like a *poodoodle!!!*'

'Now don't be silly, Eric,' said George, 'Come down here. Every cat knows how fur can stick up from time to time, and also that it is exceedingly easy, with minimal effort, to flatten it back into place.'

Eric jumped down off the wall. He had never been so embarrassed and ashamed in all his life – which rather demolished George's theory that he had no shame at all.

And what George had said about the colour of his fur was true. It was now long and fluffy, yes, but there was also the most brilliant white – not grey – mixed in with the black.

'I didn't never fink I was so whitey-white neither!' said Eric, admiring his own paws.

'Mais oui, et peut-être,' said François, 'I sink Eric, he eez 'ave a leetle beet – un petit peu – de La Perse in 'im, non? Ow you say – Persie?'

'*Persian,*' corrected George.

'Eric, you're a Persian cat!' miaowed Dog in wonder, yapping excitedly and wagging his tail (he just couldn't help it)!

'Bloomin' 'eck!' said Eric, amazed, 'There's me finkin' I's just a common old moggy, and 'ere I is some Persian pedigree pussycat!'

'Now don't get carried away,' said George, 'that's bad for a cat. François said a *little bit* Persian, not pedigree.'

But the stray wasn't listening – he was admiring his newly beautiful black-and-white fur with his one good eye (which, Eric was prepared to admit, had never seen anything quite like it).

'Now come on cats – let's continue our thorough clean, and we'll soon have Eric's fur licked into shape. Kitten – you start at the front with the whiskers. François, you do the tricky delicate underside bits – and I'll start at the back. Begin!'

Within a few moments, Eric was back to his usual shaggy long-haired self. But this time as a clean and brilliantly white-and-black part-Persian cat, and not in the slightest bit grey. Though, as George often wisely said – *'All cats are grey in the dark'* – which sounded like it meant something deep and meaningful, only Eric hadn't quite worked out exactly what yet.

All the cats admired how handsome this new and clean Eric looked, and thought with pride upon their victory that day. But for George in particular, it was charged with some sadness, as Miss Fifi was not there with them to enjoy the happy moment.

Dog miaowed at Eric, trying as hard as he could not to yap or wag his tail: he was definitely getting better at behaving like a proper and well-mannered feline. He had learnt so much from George and the others, and hoped that he would continue to learn more – and that the old tom would be willing to teach him. The cat called Dog wanted to know *everything.*

'George,' said Eric.

'Yes, Eric,' said George.

'Ain't we forgotten somefink?'

George thought as hard as he could but couldn't remember anything he'd forgotten.

'A *stiffy cat!*'

George furrowed his ginger brow into a scowl of total incomprehension.

'A *what?*' he said.

'Y'know, a *stiffy cat!* When you does a course, like, and gets a *heducation*, you gets a *stiffy cat*. Thass what I's been told any 'ow. So, the kitten-cat needs a *stiffy cat!*'

'Oh, a *certificate!*' said George, with a shake of his weary head, 'If you insist, I suppose. I do so wish you'd learn to speak proper Cat instead of that awful street dialect. It lowers the tone.'

Eric prowled away, sniffing around in search of something – though what exactly, only he knew.

'Mais oui,' said François, 'Zer petit chat, he 'as finish zer course maintenant, non?'

'Well, yes, I suppose he has, the basics anyway – part one, as it were,' said George, 'Though as a fully functioning, conscientious and cultured cat one can naturally always be adding to one's education and skills, and moreover practising what one has already learnt on a regular basis.'

'Oh I practise a lot – look!' and Dog licked his paws and gave his ears a wash standing in a most elegant feline pose.

'Splendid, kitten,' said George, 'and well done for completing the *first* part of the course. There are further parts, naturally, but you have passed part one. Congratulations!'

'Oh… thank you,' said Dog, prouder than he'd ever been, and all the cats miaowed their congratulations and clapped – (as much as they could with soft fluffy paws, anyway), 'We can award you your certificate later.'

'No need,' said Eric, 'This'll do.'

He dropped something at George's feet.

It was an empty, slightly crumpled envelope that Eric had retrieved from a bin and on which were written the words '*On Her Majesty's Service*' – (it seems tax demands did have their uses, after all).

Dog poked out his tongue proudly, and George, though he was inwardly against the idea, decided to go along with it for the sake of the kitten, who seemed very excited indeed at the thought of his '*stiffy cat.*'

He had worked so hard at being a cat – with significant, though not total, success.

And who could forget the exceptional bravery he displayed in the execution of George's plan to save The Lady from an unthinkable fate?

'It ain't got no paw print though!' miaowed Eric, so George obliged, pressing his foot into the damp wormy earth of a flowerbed before leaving his mark on the envelope.

'Congratulations, kitten-cat,' said George, dropping the certificate at Dog's feet, 'You have now officially passed part one of the course and are ready to take your superior and well-deserved place at the apex of inter-species animal society as a fully-functioning, successful and proper cat – provided you agree to study part two, that is.'

'Oh yes, I do,' miaowed Dog, the well-deserved pride of a species swelling in his chest.

George gave Dog a lick of congratulations – and thanks too – between his black pointy ears.

'Top *stiffy cat*, kitten!' miaowed Eric, wiping a tear – or perhaps an insect – away from his eye with a whiter-than-white fluffy paw, 'Bring out the biscuits!'

'Bravo, mon petit!' miaowed François, remembering his youth with a wistful, melancholy and distant stare of his sad sea-green eyes.

Dog felt so proud – it was the best day of his life by far and one he would never forget.

George sighed. It had turned out to be such a marvellous day – it was just a shame that Miss Fifi was not there to see it.

But then, a miracle happened – the like of which George had never known before in all his long, lucky, tom-cat life.

'Mademoiselle Fifi!' miaowed François in delight – because there, sashaying along the garden wall, was the slender black body of Fifi, slinking along gracefully, the very image of a cat no less liquid than its shadow.

Fifi was not dead! She had not been *'putted-down'* as François would say; she had not been *'dead-ified'* as Eric had feared.

No – Fifi was very much alive and back where she belonged!

'Miss Fifi!' miaowed George, his ebullience bounding his not inconsiderable frame over towards the wall, 'You're not... I mean... You're all better!'

Fifi purruped a purry-miaow of pleasure at being alive.

'But how... where... why... ?' said George, and then he saw the shaved patch on the flank of Fifi's body, and some awful wound there too which had been stitched.

'The brutes!' he growled, 'The place of smells and pain! Remember, kitten-cat, never go there.'

'Mais Georges, Mademoiselle Fifi she 'as been *make-ed* better, n'est-ce pas?'

This was true. George remembered how very ill Fifi looked before she was taken away by the two-legs. Now she looked as beautiful and healthy as ever, her fur as soft and smooth as before (except for the bald patch), her emerald eyes once again pools of beauty and enchantment.

'Cor blimey, she's been *better-ified!*' miaowed Eric.

'It's true, George,' said Dog, 'Miss Fifi went to 'the place of smells and pain', and came back well again.'

George thought for a moment.

Could it be that he was wrong? Could it be that 'the place of smells and pain' had saved Fifi – and what the two-legs did there was for the benefit of cats and not to bring them harm?

'Zut alors!' said François, 'I sink zat we must not to say zat name any more… we must to sink of zer uzzer name.'

'But what *other* name?' said George.

It had always been called 'the place of smells and pain' since he could remember. What else could it be?

Suddenly, Eric began jumping up and down excitedly like the most ill-mannered kitten.

'I got it!' he said, 'We could call it the place of smells and pain… and *joyfulness-ness and better-fication!*'

'Steady on, Eric,' said George, shaking his whiskers at the mangled Cat grammar, 'No need to go over the top.'

'Or *under zer bottom!*' added François, 'I sink zat we must to call ziss place zer place of smells and pain… and *Life!*'

'The place of smells and pain… and *Life*?' wondered George.

'Ah oui!' said François, 'Mademoiselle Fifi, she 'as zer life, non?'

'Miaow-prrrup-purrrup,' said Fifi, as enchantingly as ever.

'Oh yes, I agree,' said Dog – he thought it was the *purr-fect* name.

'I know!' suggested Eric, 'Seein' as this 'ere's a fing what is known as a *'cat-ocracy'* – where all cats is *hequal*, like – I fink we should 'ave a show o' paws!'

George wasn't at all sure he liked the sound of that. It was his garden, after all, and surely that made him more equal than others?

In fact, he wasn't even sure what a *'cat-ocracy'* was –

and if he wasn't sure, then it was clear as sky water that a barely educated stray like Eric wouldn't have a clue – he'd probably just picked up the word, together with a good few fleas, from some passing troublemaker.

But there are times in a cat's life when tolerance of one's inferiors is called for, if only in the name of politeness and harmony – times when one should, despite reservations, *let sleeping cats lie*.

And so, against his better instincts, and swallowing his pride like a spider, George expressed agreement with Eric:

'We need to vote on the matter,' he said, with necessary decorum – whilst almost biting his tongue with his tightly clenched jaws.

It was thus agreed that the place where Fifi had been shaved and *better-ified* would from hence forward be known as 'the place of smells and pain and *Life!*'

Just then, The Lady came out of the house calling George's name.

'The Lady!' he miaowed, happier than he had been for some considerable while.

He looked back at Miss Fifi, and she purruped her permission for George to leave her and go to The Lady.

Delighted at life, he bounded off down the garden path as fast as his plumpity would let him, into the kitchen and up into the arms of his one true love – the two-legs it was his duty to protect, look after and make happy.

George was now purring so loudly that Miss Fifi could hear the purrs from the end of the garden.

Dog followed George into the house when The Lady called him too – though she called him 'Little One' rather than 'Dog'. Then she gave them both great big bowls full of food: roast chicken flavour – George's favourite.

Eric was reluctant to enter the house, so The Lady – kind two-legs that she was – placed another large bowl (this one full of delicious biscuits) at the end of the garden. Soon he, François and Fifi were enjoying a well-deserved treat.

'Bring out the biscuits!' spluttered Eric, mid-crunch, completely ignoring cat decorum and miaowing with his mouth full.

He knew it would all work out alright in the end. Everything does, if you wait long enough – and as a stray he knew that more than most.

The Lady looked down at Dog in the kitchen, his tongue poking out its pinkness in celebration at the turn of events. He gazed up at her and – despite everything, all his lessons, all his education – yapped and wagged his tail in happiness as hard as he could, licking her hand with a purr when she picked him up in her arms.

'You know what I think?' she said, 'I think you haven't got a home to go to, have you? So I think we can adopt you, can't we, George? To say thank you, for everything. How about that, little cat?'

When Dog heard this he yapped so hard with happiness that he thought he would burst. But what about George? Dog really didn't want to tread on his tail.

George thought for a moment, twitched his whiskers and ears, and sneezed. Then he looked up at the kitten-cat – and The Lady – and miaowed his avuncular approval.

There was, he explained, nothing he would like more than some help with his strenuous house-cat duties from a young and eager kitten-cat – and it would be rather handy to have another cat around to scratch, lick and conscientiously groom his back fur to the requisite standard too.

'That's settled then, boys. We'll think of a name for you later, little kitten.'

'It's Dog,' said Dog, 'and I am a cat!'

But The Lady didn't understand his miaowing and yapping: two-legs really aren't very good at understanding other species' languages at the best of times – (but then apparently they're not all that good at understanding their own most of the time either…).

'You know,' said The Lady, 'I sometimes think George gets a bit lonely out there in the garden all day long by himself. So it'd be lovely for him to have a bit of company.'

On hearing this, George's face assumed the cat expression which is the feline equivalent of rolling one's eyes.

Life for him lately had been so hectic and action-packed that he would dearly love to spend a considerable amount of time in his garden, all by himself, alone and undisturbed in slumbering solitude – just to recover from all the recent exertions and hullabaloo.

If he were honest with himself, he was greatly looking forward to some peace and quiet after all the stress and activity of his busy schedule of late. He was exceedingly sleep-deprived and so would need at least seventeen hours of rest per day (perhaps more) from this point on in order to help him recuperate and recharge his cat batteries.

But, George being George – (and a politer cat it was not possible to know) – he did not complain at the two-legs' lack of understanding – just as he never did at their unerring ability to get *the wrong end of the tail*. He simply gave a low accepting miaow of resignation at the quaint two-legs' ignorance on display.

The most important thing was that The Lady was very sweet indeed, and he loved her – and he really did *love* her – more than anything else in the whole wide world.

The Lady put Dog down and picked up George who was, she thought, purring more loudly than he had ever done before.

'But no-one will ever replace you, George,' she said, kissing his furry ginger head, 'What a beautiful pussycat you are!'

George gazed into The Lady's eyes and purred magnificently.

'By my paws, I am a lucky cat,' he whispered.

'Splendid!' miaowed the kitten-cat from the floor – because it was.

Eric, François and Fifi watched from the garden, and Dog gave a little yelp of pleasure, happy in his new home, sure that they would all be friends *fur-ever*.

He was now officially a cat – a proper cat with a two-legs to care for and a home which had lots of warm places to curl up in too. A cat with a future.

Dog and George were by now exhausted after what had been a very busy day indeed, so found a dark carpeted corner to retire to – after miaowing goodnight to The Lady, as well as the cats outside, of course. Tiredness is no excuse for a lack of feline manners, as George had taught Dog on more than one occasion.

The kitten did his pre-sleep wash and then turned around to tell George how grateful he was for all his help. But the old ginger tom was already fast asleep and snoring, his nose and whiskers tucked under his paws, his face a *purrr-fect* picture of feline peace.

So instead, Dog gave George's head a loving lick of thanks and then flicked a final little swish of his white-tipped tail – (and a swish is hardly a wag at all, really) – and settled down to sleep, curled up next to the most marvellous and magnificent cat he had ever known.

It was a *purrr-fect* end to what had turned out to be a *purrr-fect* day.

And Dog was now, officially, and very definitely, a cat – a cat called Dog.

And he was happy with that too, though there were so many things he still wanted to ask his tutor.

But for now, at least, it was best to let one particular sleeping cat lie.

Tomorrow was another day.

'But then, it always is really, isn't it?' yawned Dog, as he snuggled up to George and fell into a deep sleepy dream.